Cursed
is the worst

A MYTHMATCHED
STORY

E.J. RUSSELL

Cursed is the Worst
Copyright © 2021 by E.J. Russell

Cover art: L.C. Chase, http://lcchase.com
Edited by Meg DesCamp

ISBN: 978-1-947033-94-8

First edition
January 2022

Contact information:
ejr@ejrussell.com

Cursed is the worst

A MYTHMATCHED STORY

E.J. RUSSELL

Chapter One

Light Fantastic.

Kiran gazed at the sign above the dance studio's door, clutching his cell phone. The digital coupon for a three-lesson social dance package was queued up, ready for a swipe of his finger.

Assuming I don't drop the phone mid-swipe. It had happened before. Multiple times. In fact, his current iPhone's screen had a crack running diagonally across one corner, which *wasn't* supposed to happen with the current model, especially not when it was protected by the industrial-strength case Kiran always bought for his hapless phones.

It's not the phone that's hapless. He frowned. Was there such a thing as hap*ful*? What was *hap* anyway? He shuffled to the edge of the sidewalk and closed the dance coupon so he could look up *hapless* on the Merriam-Webster site. Strictly for research purposes, of course. Not because he was grasping at any excuse to avoid walking through that door and prove exactly what a mistake his sister had made, insisting that Kiran, not their father, would dance with her at her wedding.

Aha! There *was* such a thing as *hap*. From the Old Norse, meaning *good luck*. Kiran's family roots were Dutch, so maybe that was why his *hap* quotient was nil.

He glanced at the studio's plate glass door with the silhouette of a male dancer mid-grand-jeté and snorted. *Hap to anybody trying to teach* me *to do that. Double hap. Maybe triple.*

But Kiran didn't want to be a dancer and never had. That was Annemiek's world. He only wanted to be able to partner her in that wedding dance without stepping on her toes or knocking her on her tail. Prima ballerinas endured enough physical stress without being bulldozed by graceless brothers.

He studied his phone screen again and winced. *Hapless: unfortunate; unlucky; jinxed.* Yikes, *that* was a little too close for comfort, although it wasn't precisely a jinx that had turned Kiran into the only clumsy swan shifter in history.

It was a curse. A curse he'd invoked with his eyes open, more or less, so he could hardly blame anybody else, could he? He sighed as he stepped toward the door—and bumped into a passerby who should have been safely out of Kiran's way.

Being cursed was the worst.

"Dude!" the man barked. "Watch where you're going."

"Sorry!" Kiran stumbled to the side and bumped into another pedestrian. "Sorry!"

When the first guy he'd caromed into narrowed his eyes, ostentatiously brushing at his jacket sleeve, Kiran offered him a tight smile and retreated to the curb, trying to will himself to be as small as possible. Not easy for a guy who was packing more than a few extra pounds. True, he'd had years of practice, but that practice didn't always translate to uncontrolled environments like sidewalks. He eyed the Light Fantastic window. *Or dance studios.*

The problem was that he *had* been watching where he was going. But it never made any difference. If somebody or something was within five feet of him, somehow their trajectories would intersect. As if their specific gravity sucked him into their orbit and straight into a collision course.

He'd known better than to even *think* about learning to drive.

But this wasn't about him. This was about Annemiek and making her wedding as perfect as she dreamed it would be.

So Kiran waited until the sidewalk was clear by at least ten feet in either direction and then lunged for the studio door, breathing a sigh of relief when he grasped the handle without further unfortunate impacts. He peered through the glass at a small lobby clustered with neat racks of dance apparel and posters of dancers on the walls. He couldn't help a smile when he spotted one of Annemiek in her signature *Firebird* role. When she'd joined New Repertory Ballet, she'd made it a stipulation in her contract that she was *never* to dance Odette/Odile in *Swan Lake*.

"Let the other dancers think it's because I can't handle Odette's thirty-two fouettés in Act III. You and I know the truth, right, Kir?"

The truth was that Annemiek refused to be a cliché. A swan shifter playing a swan shifter? Too on the nose by half.

That poster made it seem like fate that Kiran had found his way here unscathed (relatively), that Light Fantastic was the perfect choice. He only hoped that the studio name didn't hint at anything remotely prophetic and that he wouldn't *trip*—over his own feet, over the instructor's, over *nothing*.

"There's a first time for everything, right?"

He shoved at the door. It didn't move. Frowning, he shoved again. Still nothing. Then he saw the word in four-inch high letters above the handle: PULL. *Heh*. Nerves. That's all it was. Kiran could compensate perfectly well for his physical ineptitude with *planning*, but he wasn't so great at *improvising*. His whole reason for being here was an impulse. He'd been on the verge of calling Annemiek—and possibly breaking her heart or disappointing Del, her spouse-to-be, who'd apparently suggested Kiran lead her in the dance in the first place.

"Del says it should be you," Annemiek had said, "and who are you going to listen to, if not an oracle?"

Kiran had his doubts, but when he'd asked Del if they were sure, Del had simply smiled. They were ruthlessly efficient—a skill they needed as the manager of Hunter's Moon, a rock band consisting of two werewolves, a jaguar shifter, a kangaroo shifter, and the last true bard of Faerie —but they had a definite weakness: Annemiek. If she had even hinted that something would make her happy, Del would move heaven, earth, Sheol, *and* Faerie to make it happen.

But as he'd been about to make the call to pull out in favor of their father, a little toast had popped up on Kiran's computer screen, right above the stock ticker app:

We'll make you dance-floor ready in three lessons or your money back.

For Annemiek, Kiran had decided to give it one more shot. All he had to do was *PULL.*

So he did, stepping into a tiny vestibule, its inner door propped wide, and from there into the lobby. Instead of the usual industrial fluorescents, the room was bathed in indirect light from the soffits near the ceiling. It was softer, easier on the eyes, but still bright enough to illuminate the colorful clothing on sale. Each poster seemed highlighted by its own little spotlight, but Kiran couldn't figure out how, since there didn't seem to be any mounted on the acoustic ceiling tiles.

"Hello. May I help you?"

Kiran whirled at the sound of an impossibly deep voice, whacking his elbow on a circular rack of tiny tutus and sending it tottering. He grabbed at it, only succeeding in knocking it completely off balance. Before it could crash to the floor in a flutter of pink tulle, though, a large brown hand caught it deftly and set it upright.

"I'm so sorry," Kiran said. "I didn't think I was close enough to…to…" His voice failed as he gazed up at the man who'd rescued the tutus from certain death. He was taller than Kiran by a good three inches, his chest broad under his snug, gray *Light Fantastic* T-shirt and taut with the kind of muscles that lifted other dancers, not weights. The smooth brown dome of his head glowed in the indirect lighting. Either he shaved his head or was naturally bald, but on him it was definitely a mouthwatering look. His dark brown eyes crinkled at the corners and his full lips were framed by a closely trimmed goatee.

"You look just like Taye Diggs in *Chicago*," Kiran blurted, and then felt heat rushing up his throat. "Sorry. Usually I'm not quite as clumsy verbally as I am physically."

The man chuckled, a low purr that hit Kiran right in the belly and spread out from there. "No worries." He gestured to the tutu rack. "And no harm done. I'm Taj Sekani, owner of Light Fantastic. How may I help you today?"

Kiran forced himself not to get lost in Taj's smile, although it was a struggle. Working from his home office as he did, communicating more with numbers, financial reports, and investment recommendations, the only people he saw regularly—he didn't count the people he ran into whenever he ventured outside—were Annemiek, Del, and his father, and the skies knew his father hadn't smiled at him since he was ten years old.

He fumbled with his phone, losing his grip on it only to have Taj catch it and return it to him with the grace of a true dancer. "Th-thanks." He retrieved the coupon and turned the screen toward Taj. "I'm here for the social dance package. But I need to cram all three lessons in before Saturday. Do you have time on your schedule to fit me in?"

Taj's left eyebrow twitched as he glanced at Kiran's phone, but he said, "Of course." He gestured to a door on one side of the small reception area. "Join me in Studio A?"

"O-Okay." Kiran gulped. He hadn't expected to start *now*. He thought he'd have more time to prepare, to brace himself. But Saturday—the wedding—was only five days away. He really didn't have time to lose. "That works."

"I will need one thing, however."

"Of course." Kiran reached for his wallet. "Is cash all right?"

Taj stopped him with a touch to his shoulder. "Not your money, my friend." He smiled again and winked. "Your name."

"Oh." Kiran laughed weakly. "I'm Kiran. Kiran Bakker."

"I'm pleased to meet you, Kiran." He gestured for Kiran to precede him into the room with its gleaming wood floors and—gods—mirrored wall. "Shall we?"

Taj forbore from mentioning that he'd have no trouble fitting Kiran into his schedule since Light Fantastic had no students scheduled at all, and hadn't since it opened a month ago. Nobody had so much as called, let alone crossed the threshold. Every class so far had consisted of him in an echoingly empty room, staring into the mirror as music whispered from the sound system.

To soothe himself, or perhaps out of his innate demon stubbornness, Taj had kept the music keyed to the published session content—ballet, jazz, Broadway, hip-hop, ballroom, tap—and had gone through warm-up, technique, and choreography as if he had actual students following his instructions.

Dancing with myself. He'd had no choice. It was as though nobody could even see the studio, his website, his ads. As though he were as invisible as any captive soul.

Yet here was this man, neatly dressed in polo and khakis, with his wavy dark blond hair and neatly trimmed beard, his diffident smile and hopeful gray eyes, holding a coupon Taj had never seen before.

There was no way in Sheol that Taj would turn this man away or pretend that the promotion wasn't his own idea.

He'd worry about where it came from later.

For now, he had a student, and from the way this student—*Kiran*—kept his arms tucked close to his sides and his shoulders hunched, Kiran had serious doubts about Taj's credentials and ability to help him.

Taj kept his thoughts trapped behind a smile he'd had centuries to perfect, because Kiran had every reason for doubt. Since the moment Naberius, his demon progenitor, had manifested him, the only *help* Taj had offered came with strings—strings of the soul-selling variety.

Those days were gone, however. With the Realm Accords, Taj had every right to seek his fortune here in the Upper World, free to live his own life at last.

The catch, of course, was that in addition to *seeking* his fortune, he had to actually *find* it, at least enough of it to prove he could support himself in the human realm. Unless a few more students miraculously discovered his studio and clamored for his instruction, he'd be broke and back in Sheol before Samhain.

Never. No matter what I have to do, I'm never going back.

Then Taj caught Kiran's almost imperceptible sigh and the resignation that flitted across his face. Perhaps his doubts were about his own abilities and not Taj's at all.

"I assure you," Taj said, "there's no judgment here. I assume no prior experience or skill level." He placed a hand under Kiran's elbow to guide him into the dance room and to one of the chairs that lined the side wall. "Why don't you tell me what you'd like to accomplish with your lessons? Since you have a timeline, I assume you have a goal in mind?"

"Yes. Well. My sister is getting married on Saturday, and she wants me to partner her in the first dance after the one with her new spouse." He smiled crookedly and Taj's heart—which he'd been certain had solidified into an unfeeling cinder centuries ago—gave an odd, sideways thump, as if it had been shocked into beating again.

To cover the unexpected feeling, he cleared his throat. "Forgive me if I'm touching on a sensitive subject, but isn't that dance usually reserved for a parent? If you've lost yours, I'm sorry—"

"No, no." Kiran folded his hands in his lap, fingers whitening with the force of his grip, and Taj's heart stuttered again. "It's fine. We lost our mother years ago, but my father is very much alive, and not happy with Annemiek's choice, so—

"Annemiek?" Taj held up a hand. "Pardon me for interrupting, but you said your last name was Bakker? Annemiek Bakker is not that common a name, at least not here in the United States."

That lopsided smile was going to be the death of Taj. He'd need a pacemaker by the time Kiran's lessons were over.

"If you're asking whether my sister is the same Annemiek Bakker whose poster you've got on your wall, the answer is yes. As you can tell by"—he gestured toward the lobby—"Anni got all the grace in our family and I muddle through as best I can."

"Your sister is brilliant, yes." To distract himself from his reaction to Kiran's nearness—his scent, like forest and lake, so different from Sheol's sulfur and brimstone; his eyes, so clear and kind; his shape, solid and warm and real—he winked again. "Can I confess I prefer her

Coppelia to her Firebird? And that I'm one of the legions of ballet fans who have been crying out for her to dance *Swan Lake?*"

Kiran chuckled, for the first time not looking nervous. "That will never happen." Then he glanced away almost furtively. "She, um, has her reasons."

"Of course. As do we all." Taj studied Kiran's feet. "While running shoes might be acceptable for hip-hop, I'll make a leap of logic and guess that's not what you hope to master by Saturday?"

"No. Gods, no," Kiran said. "Just...I don't know...a fox trot? A basic box step?" His eyes widened. "Not a waltz, because the possibilities for death and untold destruction if I get dizzy are simply too great."

Taj chuckled. "I doubt the results would be quite so dire."

"You have no idea," Kiran muttered.

"However, since you're only concerned with a single dance on a single day, we'd be better off focusing on that specifically. Do you know what music will be played for the dance?"

Kiran blinked, as though it had never occurred to him before. "I...never asked. But I'm sure Anni knows. Or Del, her spouse-to-be. They know everything, and anyway, the band they manage will be playing at the reception."

"You needn't trouble them now, but perhaps for our first lesson, you could get the music from them? We could then choreograph the dance and practice it." Taj spread his hands. "Not even your sister, as gifted as she is, could perform flawlessly without rehearsal. So that is what we will do."

Chapter Two

Rehearsal. That was like planning and preparation, right? Those Kiran could do. He'd had the two decades since the curse to carve a life for himself that didn't depend on large motor skills or spatial awareness to achieve success. He'd found that breaking tasks down into manageable components and *practicing* was the way to go.

It didn't guard against unexpected close encounters with random passersby, or tripping over his shoes if he'd forgotten to put them safely away when he took them off. But he'd arranged his condo—spare yet comfortable; all decor relegated to the walls; desk with its multiple monitors tucked safely into the corner—so that he could navigate successfully. He managed to cook his own meals and make his own coffee, as long as he wasn't trying to multi-task or move around too much in the process.

"Anni and Del are both traveling today, so I don't know if I can reach them right now to ask about the music." He worried his lower lip. "I hate to waste today's lesson, but —"

"Oh, this doesn't count as part of the package," Taj said with that devastating grin. "This is a pre-lesson consultation. Preparation, if you will. Today's Monday, so we can schedule your three sessions for tomorrow,

Wednesday, and Thursday. Unless you'd rather keep the last one closer to the event?"

"No. I'll be traveling to the venue on Friday afternoon, so let's plan to finish up on Thursday." That would give him a chance to practice more on his own. A couple dozen repeats in his uncluttered living room should solidify the moves in his mind. He gazed into Taj's eyes. *That's one place I wouldn't mind falling.* Although a fall into those dark eyes might be just as devastating as tripping over the curb or colliding with a streetlamp.

Because a swan shifter like Kiran—a member of the supernatural community, a supe—couldn't risk a relationship with a human, not without threatening the Secrecy Pact, the rules that all supernatural races agreed to abide by for their own safety. Besides, *Swan Lake* was a perfect example of why swans in particular needed to stay far away from humans.

"Did you have another question?" Taj asked in that honey-velvet voice.

"Did I? Oh. Sorry. Yes, I did. Even if we rehearse the choreography together, what about Anni? If she doesn't know the steps…"

Taj chuckled again and *oooh* what that did to Kiran's nerves. "I'll video our final session so you can send it to her. She's a professional. She'll be able to pick it up in no time." He winked again. "It's not like we'll be breaking out the grand pas from *Nutcracker Suite.*"

Just the thought of what a shambles Kiran would make out of *that*, the steps as well as his hapless partner's body —and anybody partnering with Kiran would be the definition of *hapless*—was enough to send his belly into a downward spiral. "Don't even joke about that."

Taj's smile faded. "I beg your pardon. I have no intention of mocking you. But dancing should bring joy, more so to those who dance than for those who are watching. In this instance, the only people you need to worry about pleasing are yourself and your sister. If she loves you enough to want you, above all others in the world, to dance with her at her wedding, then she cares more about the connection between you than what any other guest will think."

"A nice sentiment, but you haven't met my father or the honor attendant's mother." Kiran shuddered. No matter how much rehearsal he logged, he could never meet Carolee McIlhenny's exacting standards. A transplanted southern belle, she was the quintessential dance mom. Her daughter, Sandrine, Annemiek's best friend since kindergarten, hadn't let her helicopter mother affect her, though, ignoring Carolee's passive-aggressive remarks and embarking happily on a career in arts administration rather than professional dance.

"If they're so judgmental, then I'm glad I haven't." Taj slapped his knees. "Now, let's prepare for your lessons, shall we? For the first two, I'd like to you wear comfortable workout gear. Since you're not about to take the stage in Matthew Bourne's *Swan Lake*, I'm not concerned too much about line and form, so your clothes needn't be close fitting. But you should be able to move easily in them. What are you wearing to the wedding?"

"A tux."

"A tux," Taj said, his tone doubtful. "Does it fit you well?"

Kiran lifted an eyebrow. "Are you asking whether or not it's a rental?"

Taj's grin flashed, nearly melting Kiran's bones. "Should I work on my subtlety?"

"Not at all. It was smooth. Very smooth. And no, it's not a rental. It's bespoke."

He nodded, as if in approval. "Black?"

"Yes."

"Shoes?"

"The, uh, patent leather kind. Shiny."

"Hmmm." Taj's eyes narrowed. "That might do for the rest of the festivities, but for the dance, particularly if you're worried about...unfortunate events, you need proper dance shoes."

"I, um, like *your* shoes."

Taj grinned, probably recognizing the deflection for what it was. "So do I. They're magical."

Magical shoes. If only Kiran could find such a thing. Then he could avoid the pain of the upcoming awkward lessons as well as not ruin Annemiek's wedding. But he knew better than to expect miracles.

"Do I really need special shoes? I don't have time to shop for them." He had quarterly investment reports to prepare for several clients by Friday morning, so he could leave for the wedding venue that afternoon. "I wouldn't even know where to look."

"No need to look any farther than right here." Taj pointed to the floor with both index fingers. "I sell appropriate shoes for all the dance styles I teach." He slipped from his chair to kneel gracefully in front of Kiran, his hands hovering over the instep of Kiran's right foot. "May I? I need to measure your feet to determine the best fit."

Kiran nodded, his throat suddenly tight. And then Taj's hands were on his foot and he thought he might actually pass out. Because other than Annemiek, nobody had touched him that gently since his mother's death. And gods preserve him, but Kiran wanted more, wanted to feel Taj's arms around him at least once.

If that meant he had to endure the potential disaster of a dance lesson, it would be so worth it. He set his jaw, ignoring the danger klaxons blaring in his mind.

Bring it on.

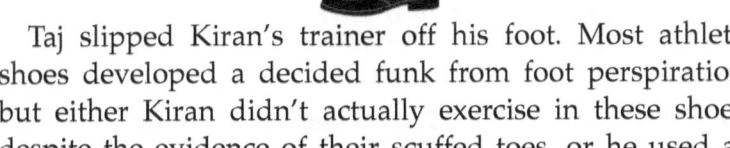

Taj slipped Kiran's trainer off his foot. Most athletic shoes developed a decided funk from foot perspiration, but either Kiran didn't actually exercise in these shoes, despite the evidence of their scuffed toes, or he used an industrial strength foot powder. Because the only scent wafting off his shoe was a faint whiff of cut grass.

The man's feet were a lovely shape, even inside a dreadful bulky tube sock that should be illegal. High arches, sloping instep, narrow heel. For some reason, holding Kiran's foot felt like holding a bird about to take flight. Taj didn't stop to think about where that notion had come from. "May I remove your sock?"

"Uh..."

Taj glanced up at the strained note in Kiran's voice. "I'm sorry. Am I hurting you?"

"No," he croaked. "Not at all." His smile was forced, though, and Taj winced internally. Not everyone could handle having their feet...well...handled.

"Are you sure? Because if this makes you uncomfortable, I don't have to—"

"No!" Kiran sucked in a breath. "I mean, I'm not uncomfortable. But my feet aren't exactly lovely. I, um, stub my toes a lot."

Oh, if that's *all.* "I've been a dancer for years." Taj grinned up at him. "Your own sister is a ballerina, so you, more than anyone, should know that a dancer will never pass judgment on the state of anybody else's feet. I only want to make sure I select the right shoe for your foot shape."

"Don't you need one of those foot measuring gadgets? Like in the shoe store?"

Taj held up one hand, fingers spread. "This is the gadget I use." That was one of the abilities Naberius had baked into him, the better to steer an unwilling victim to shoes that were just this side of excruciating. More dancers than Taj could count were willing to sell their souls for shoes that didn't hurt. "You won't be wearing socks this thick at the wedding, correct?"

Kiran huffed a laugh. "Anni would kill me. No. I just wear these for the extra padding."

"To cushion against toe stubs?"

"Exactly." He made a *go ahead* gesture with both hands. "But I can stand the sight if you can."

"Very well then." Taj slid the offensive sock off, noticing as he did so that it was dry and blindingly white. Underneath, Kiran's foot was pale, the skin remarkably smooth across the instep. No corns or bunions. Taj turned it gently to study the sole. No calluses on heel or ball, although Kiran kept his toes tightly clenched together. "Do your toes hurt?"

"Not at the moment."

"I'll have a better idea of your shoe size if you relax them a trifle."

Kiran took a shaky breath. "All right. But no judgment, right?"

"Never." That was above Taj's pay grade. Judgment had always been reserved for the C-suite demons, or middle management like Naberius at the least.

Taj felt the moment Kiran let go, because an odd tingle zinged through his fingers and up his arm. It was his turn to suck in a breath, but he covered it. He hoped. But when Kiran sighed and tensed again, he figured he'd failed.

"It's a shock, I know," Kiran said resignedly.

You have no idea. "I'm not shocked in the least." *And I'm a lying liar who lies.* But then, that skill had been baked into him by Naberius too.

"Oh really?" Kiran's tone was decidedly tart. "You see webbed toes every day and twice on Sunday, I suppose."

"Webbed toes?" Taj tore his gaze off Kiran's face and studied his feet. Kiran had spread his toes and sure enough, there was a hint of webbing at their base. "Actually, this isn't that unusual. The metatarsal membranes have a wide range of what's considered ordinary." He smiled. "You needn't be self-conscious about your toes. In fact, any dancer would be proud to have feet as lovely as yours."

"Lovely." Kiran snorted. "Right."

Taj gave him a mock-severe glare. "Hey. Who's the professional here? I know what I'm talking about." He stood. "And I know exactly the size and style of shoe that will suit you. I'll be right back."

He made himself stride out of the room, brisk and businesslike, thanking every power in existence that the dance belt he was wearing under his jazz pants did a better-than-average job masking his hardening cock.

What was *wrong* with him? He wasn't an incubus, to be beguiled by life energies. Yes, he was fully functional—Naberius hadn't wanted to close off any potential temptation paths for his victims—but seduction hadn't usually been Taj's purview. He was built to encourage *professional* envy and jealousy, not physical lust.

In all the centuries that Taj had been Naberius's minion, he'd *never* felt attraction to another person for his own sake. He couldn't. He'd assumed that Naberius had left the emotional capacity out of his makeup for fear it would interfere with hooking the intended victim.

He shook his head. He doubted Naberius, as self-centered as he was, would have been thoughtful enough to spare his minion the inconvenience of empathy, guilt, and—yes—hope. Because Taj had hoped in vain every single time he'd worked their target up to the state where they were primed for Naberius's infernal proposal. Hoped the victim would say no, would refuse the offer of success, of renown, of adulation.

But eternal torment at some vague future date never outweighed the immediate lure of fame and fortune, and all of them—every single one without exception—had taken the deal and paid the price. Over the years, Taj had learned to steel himself against remorse for the part he played in Naberius's schemes, but he'd never banished it completely.

That was one of the reasons Taj was desperate to make his studio pay, to prove he could support himself here in the Upper World among humans. Because if he were forced to return to Sheol, he'd hear them. All the souls he'd helped to trap, all of them begging for one more part, one more solo, one more moment under the stage lights. But that could never happen in Sheol's relentless dark.

His final hope was that, as stipulated in the Realm Accords, each of them would finally be released to move on.

He stepped into the closet, a deceptively small cubicle next to the office, and reached into the dimensional storage pocket where he kept his dance shoe stock—all sizes, colors, styles, anything his students might need, since he'd paid extra to ensure the pocket was infinitely expandable.

Unfortunately, unless he managed to pull a few *students* out of a magical hat, he'd be back in Sheol in a matter of weeks. And unlike Naberius's victims, he had no place else to go.

Chapter Three

Kiran hugged himself as he flexed his foot with its telltale toe-webbing. *He wasn't revolted.* Kiran had learned over the years, in locker rooms, on beaches, in doctors' offices, that most humans found his toes at least disturbing, if not outright ridiculous or disgusting. While he'd learned to hide them, he couldn't regret them. They were the reminder that while his curse meant he could never fly—he couldn't coordinate his wingbeats, even though before the curse, he'd been a precocious early fledgling—he could still shift to float and paddle.

Of course, before the new King of Faerie had established the FTA—Fae Transportation Association—Kiran hadn't had access to any secluded body of water where he could shift out of sight, not when he was restricted to public transportation or tagging along with Annemiek when her performance schedule allowed for a little swan time. Now, though, he could call up an FTA driver and request a trip through Faerie to any number of private lakes, including the one at the Wildwood resort where the wedding would take place.

The resort was owned by two supes—a grizzly shifter and his incubus husband—and they graciously allowed Kiran to visit and swim in the lake whenever he liked.

Although, since the resort catered to humans as well as supes, they asked him to be sure to shift out of sight in the woods.

A small price to pay.

He had unlimited access to the FTA because he'd set up their payment infrastructure for both riders and drivers. He snorted. His father might persist in viewing him as a failure, but his extensive client base had an entirely different view.

Of course, since his clients were all part of the supe community, they'd have definite opinions about Kiran's inconvenient attraction to a human dance instructor. But it was only three lessons. If his webbed toes didn't scream *inhuman*, then surely he could keep up the pretense of being equally human for three more days.

Although he felt a twinge at the thought that he'd never see Taj again after the lessons ended.

Maybe I could sign up for a regular class. He studied the schedule on the bulletin board next to his head. There were several for adults: ballet barre workout, beginning jazz, West Coast swing, introduction to hip hop.

Who am I kidding?

He was pressing his luck—and endangering *Taj's* toes— with the three-lesson package. He shuddered to think what kind of havoc he could wreak in a room full of other students.

Taj strode back into the room before Kiran could spiral any farther into desire or despair, three shoe boxes under his arm. "Here we are."

Kiran lifted an eyebrow at the boxes. "I thought you could magically tell my size."

Taj hesitated for an instant—so briefly that Kiran might have imagined it—before he smiled. "I can." He sank to the floor, landing cross-legged at Kiran's feet. "All of these will fit beautifully and feel great. They're slightly different styles, however, so I wanted to give you some options."

"Are any of them as magical as yours?"

Taj smiled at him, his teeth nearly blinding against his dark skin. "They're as magical as you make them."

Kiran snorted. "Then they'll be as mundane as paperclips."

"Nonsense." He opened the first box and lifted out an oxford-style shoe in smooth black leather that looked so soft Kiran ached to stroke it almost as much as he ached to stroke Taj's cheek. *Okay, so maybe not that much.* Taj presented Kiran with a thin black sock. "Would you like to do the honors, sock-wise?"

Kiran wanted to give in to temptation and ask Taj to slip the sock on his foot, *reeeaaally* slowly, but the poor guy would have enough to deal with once he got Kiran out on the dance floor. "Sure." He pulled on the sock, but let Taj slip on the shoe and tie its laces.

"How does that feel?"

Kiran stood, testing the shoe against the wooden floor. The sole was flexible, the uppers soft enough to hug his foot, the heel not cutting into his Achilles the way most athletic shoes did. "It feels good." Although not as good as Taj's hands on his skin.

"Let's put on its mate, and then I'll show you the other options." Kiran handled the second sock, but once again let Taj ease the shoe on. Then Taj stood and held out his hand. "Come on. Let's take them for a spin."

Kiran reared back in his chair. "What? I couldn't do that. I might injure you!"

Taj clocked him with that · devastating grin again. "You'll have to put up with me at some point, you know. Besides, dancer, remember? My feet are tough." He waggled his eyebrows. "And my shoes are magical."

"You laugh now," Kiran grumbled, "but just wait." Nevertheless, he let Taj pull him to his feet.

"Walk to the center of the room?"

Kiran eyed the expanse of gleaming wood. The center of the room was empty of obstacles, much like the rooms in his condo. He could probably manage the trip without maiming Taj or himself. He took the first step rather gingerly, but when no disaster occurred, he strode forward more confidently. When he made it to the middle of the room without tripping, he turned and beamed at Taj. "They really *are* magical!"

Taj chuckled. "Don't give them all the credit. You did the work." He took a step forward, held up both hands, and beckoned. "Now come back to me."

"You, um, might want to be ready to leap aside."

"Again, I say nonsense."

"Let it be on your head, then." Kiran walked toward Taj, gaining a little speed as he grew closer. "Hey, I'm doing—" Then he stumbled and flailed, but instead of falling on his face as usual, he landed in Taj's arms.

"Hello," Taj said, his warm tone laced with amusement, but not mockery, as he steadied Kiran within his embrace.

Kiran's face heated—as did other parts of his body. "I warned you."

"Yes, but I very craftily ignored you. My intention was to demonstrate a proper dance hold once before you left, so this…fell in perfectly with my nefarious plans." He drew Kiran closer, slotting their legs together and spun him once, twice, three times, stopping in the middle of the floor and leaving Kiran suddenly breathless. "How about that? Your first dance steps and no harm done."

Kiran gazed up into Taj's eyes, belly fluttering. *I'm not sure about that. Not sure at all.*

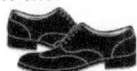

Taj's breath had caught somewhere south of his throat. "Would you like to test the other shoes?"

"No." Kiran's voice was hoarse. Throaty even? Taj could only hope. "These are perfect."

"Care to try a couple more steps while you're here?"

"If you're willing to risk it." Kiran's breathless laugh went straight to Taj's groin. *Awkward.* No dance belt was *that* powerful.

"Just to be safe, I'll, uh, put all the other pairs away."

Kiran nodded, but Taj liked to think it was with reluctance. He stepped back and turned away, quickly scooping up the unneeded boxes and hurrying out of the room. Once inside the closet, he took a moment to breathe deeply.

Control yourself, Tendaji-al-Sefu. You managed it for centuries.

Of course, the reason he'd managed for centuries was that *he* wasn't the one in control of his actions. Naberius owned him, wielded him like a weapon, aiming him at a succession of victims down the ages. The only reason Taj had any room for his own thoughts was because Naberius was fundamentally lazy and couldn't be bothered to monitor him all the time.

Had Taj always been this weak behind that control? If he hadn't had Naberius pulling his strings, would he have succumbed to attraction to an appealing human long since? He didn't *think* that was the case. For one thing, he'd had that limited free time while Naberius was off brooding about the unfairness of the universe, and he'd never been tempted before.

Not until Kiran.

Could that be because all his assignments had been people with extremely robust egos? Kiran was the first *diffident* man he'd met, the first person who wanted Taj's help for someone other than himself. Whatever the reason, Taj needed to maintain his professionalism. Jumping the bones of the first student to walk through his doors was *not* the way to establish his business.

He shoved the first shoebox into the dimensional storage pocket, but it ran into something before he could send it flying to its proper location. "What the..." That shouldn't be possible. The pocket was keyed to Taj's own magic, everything instantly storable or accessible. He tried again.

Something clamped down *hard* on his wrist.

"*Awp!*" His grip tightened on the shoebox, crumpling its cardboard top, as he braced himself and *pulled*. Whatever had his arm wasn't giving up easily, because it pulled back, and even before Taj's wrist came into view circled with a green-scaled hand, he knew who it had to be.

"Naberius," he hissed. "You have no right to invade my personal pocket."

Naberius let go and popped out of the pocket like a cork. "Nonsense. I have every right." He brushed nonexistent scale lint from his arms and stamped his hooves. "You're my minion."

"Not anymore. The Realm Accords took care of that little detail."

"Minion emeritus then, but we'll discuss that in a moment." Naberius turned in a slow circle, and given that he was wider than Taj, taller by a foot if you counted his crest, and had a beak like a Plague Doctor mask, it made the closet as cramped as an Iron Maiden. "How quaint." He flicked his claws, and the space doubled in size. "That's better."

"You can't be here. If a human should catch sight of you —"

"Oh, calm down. Do you see any humans in here? I certainly don't."

"Well, there could be." If Taj didn't get back to Kiran soon, he might come looking. And if he found Naberius here, Taj would be responsible for a major violation of the Secrecy Pact. It didn't matter that Naberius had arrived without an invitation. The studio was Taj's, therefore anything that occurred within its walls was his responsibility. "What do you want?"

"Perhaps to find out why in all the realms you want to set yourself up as a *dance teacher*."

"Maybe because I want to teach people to dance?"

Naberius gazed at the ceiling from behind thick, smoky-lensed goggles. "I don't know *what* I was thinking when I baked an actual love of the arts into your manifestation matrix."

Taj folded his arms. "You know perfectly well what you were thinking. You were thinking, 'Not only will I snag the souls of fame-seeking actors, singers, and dancers, but

I get to torment my minion too by ensuring he never gets to perform himself. Bonus!'"

"Oh. Yes." Naberius tapped his beak with one claw. "I suppose that *is* what I was thinking."

Taj had lost count of the number of times when—at Naberius's orders—he'd sprained his ankle on opening night, paving the way for the understudy to make it big, or developed laryngitis an hour before the big concert, so a previously unknown singer could take his solo and hit the big time. Being pushed out of the limelight had never bothered Taj. He'd never craved performing, not like Naberius did. He was just as happy in the audience or as a mentor or instructor. But it had always bothered him that someone would have to literally sell their soul to have their dreams come true—if only for a short while.

"Why did you hate performers so much? Why do you *still* hate performers so much?"

"None of them have my talent!" Naberius squawked, making Taj thankful he'd sprung for extra soundproofing on the studio walls. "I would have acted them off the stage, danced them to oblivion, sung them into stunned silence!"

"There's a tiny problem with that notion. You never learned to dance, your voice sounds like a whole murder of crows, and the number of roles appropriate for a seven-foot tall, green-scaled, shark-toothed, bird-headed person with cloven hooves are limited, to say the least."

"Details," Naberius grumbled. "I'll have you know my TikTok channel is *very* popular."

"So why dwell on the past? Why not leave me alone and focus on your newfound social media fame?"

He clacked his beak irritably. "Because I loathe loose ends."

Taj stared at him, nonplussed. "You do not. You've never cleaned up after yourself in your life. You always left that to me."

"Exactly."

Taj sighed. "Let me guess. Some former *client*"—he loaded his voice with irony, since every single one of them was a victim—"is claiming you didn't fulfill the contract terms so they don't have to forfeit their soul. Did you bother to tell them that all contracts were nullified after the Realm Accords?"

"I tried." Naberius sounded aggrieved, as only the truly self-absorbed could manage. "But there was enough vagueness in the original language that she claims I owe her anyway, even without the soul payment."

"Contract vagueness? You?"

"Give me a break! I was distracted. *Firefly* had just been canceled, and you *know* how much I loved Captain Tight Pants!"

"Oh, come off it. *You* were responsible for that anyway because you got all snitty when Joss Whedon refused to take a meeting with you."

Naberius's crest flattened. "I never dreamed he wouldn't take the bait," he muttered.

"It's not my problem anymore, Naberius. The Realm Accords freed me from Sheol and from you. You'll have to figure out how to tie up your loose end on your own."

"Now, now, let's not be too hasty." He leaned against the wall, rumpling his feather-trimmed toga. "I think we can come to a mutually beneficial arrangement."

Taj narrowed his eyes. "That's what you said to all of your victims, right before they signed their souls away."

His crest popped up, all its spikes erect. "Every one of those contracts was totally legit. They got exactly what was promised them." The crest drooped again. "All except this one."

"Not my problem."

Naberius's beak gaped in his version of a smirk. "Actually, it is."

Taj glanced at his watch. He'd been gone for too long. Would Kiran lose patience and leave? They hadn't scheduled his sessions yet. "I did exactly what you ordered me to do from the moment you manifested me, so you can't lay this on me."

"Oh yes," Naberius said archly. "Tendaji-al-Sefu, the perfect minion." He jabbed a claw at Taj's chest, just snagging his T-shirt. "You did the bare minimum of what I asked. Where was your initiative? Your ambition? Your creativity?"

"If I'd shown the least initiative, you'd have chucked me in the lava river for a couple of decades. Give it up, Naberius. You've got nothing on me. And by the way, you can lose the goggles. The lights in the studio are all configured for Sheol-adapted eyesight." It had cost him a huge chunk of his restitution settlement to do it, but he didn't like to wear glasses when he taught, and no demon could handle Upper World light without adaptive lenses.

Naberius ran a claw tip over the goggle straps. "I rather like them. And while I may have nothing on you, I can certainly do something *for* you. In fact, I have done." He produced a cell phone out of thin air, its screen displaying the same coupon Kiran had shown.

"*You* posted that coupon?"

"I did." Naberius preened. "You owe me your only student."

Taj's eyebrows snapped together. "How do you know he's my only student?"

"Er..." Naberius's beak clicked nervously. "Lucky guess?"

"You're masking the studio, blocking my website, aren't you? *You're* the reason the studio is circling the drain! That's completely against the restitution clause in the Realm Accords!"

"Don't be so dramatic. Do you seriously think you could start a new business in the Upper World without my help?"

Taj clenched his fists, scowling. "I'd have a much better chance if you weren't deliberately sabotaging me."

"So touchy. Look. You help me with this last little detail, and I'll lift all my little...safety checks." He leered. "And I *won't* stroll into that room and flash your only student."

"You wouldn't."

"Watch me."

Naberius flickered, a sure sign he was about to phase-shift.

Taj grabbed for him, but his hands passed right through Naberius's body, sending an unpleasant Taser-like jolt up his arms. Naberius lifted into the air and his head disappeared through the wall.

"Stop it, Naberius." Taj huffed a breath through flared nostrils. "All *right*. I'll help you. Just don't confront my student."

Naberius extracted his head and dropped to his hooves, fully corporeal once more. "That's more like it." He tilted his head, birdlike. "Now get rid of him and we'll talk details."

When Taj returned after apologizing profusely to Kiran and claiming a personal emergency—which it most certainly was—Naberius was gone.

But Taj harbored zero illusions that he wouldn't return.

Chapter Four

Clutching the Light Fantastic bag holding his new shoes, Kiran made his way to the MAX train stop, only running into one light pole and three pedestrians along the way. He tried to bury his disappointment that Taj had to cut their consultation short. He'd wanted so much to step into Taj's arms and be twirled around the room again. It had filled him with the same joy and lightness as flying before his curse had robbed him of the ability. He couldn't be resentful, though. The three-lesson package didn't say anything about a bonus consultation, so Kiran was pretty sure Taj had only done it to be nice.

But he'd see Taj again tomorrow for the first real lesson, and skies willing, he'd have another chance to *fly* again.

When Kiran got off the train—only one collision, this time with the edge of a seat—in front of his building in the Pearl District, he still hadn't returned completely to the ground. He waved at the witch who was arranging a crystal display in the window of the street-level New Age store before entering the vestibule and checking his mail. Purchasing this building and its neighbor had been one of his more successful investments. Aside from its convenience for a person who didn't and couldn't drive, he was able to rent the retail spaces to other supe businesses, eliminating certain awkwardness such businesses experienced. Explaining to a landlord why they needed to remove the windows from a room, line it with slate tiles, and embed a bronze pentagram in the floor, for instance. Human landlords were notoriously inflexible when it came to magic workroom requirements. Go figure.

As Kiran stepped into the elevator—he knew better than to trust himself on the two flights of stairs up to his unit—he detected a faint rhythmic pounding from overhead. He smiled, recognizing the sound for what it was. Sure enough, when he opened his door, his sister was sitting cross-legged in the center of his living room, whacking a toe shoe mercilessly against a special felt-covered wooden block Kiran kept just for this purpose.

"It's a good thing I invested in those special soundproofing spells," he said as he set the bag on the table in the alcove inside the door.

Annemiek looked up at him and grinned, although she didn't stop beating her shoe into submission. She'd been doing it for so many years, she barely had to pay attention anymore and could conduct entire philosophical conversations without ever losing her rhythm. "I'll bet you didn't have to pay a dime. The witches' collective probably gave them to you gratis for letting them hold their sky-clad ceremonies on the roof."

"I'll never tell," Kiran said. He stayed near the wall, well out of range of her swing. "Not that I'm not glad to see you, but I thought you and Sandrine were indulging in a girls' spa extravaganza at the Royal Sonesta for the next couple of days before you leave for Wildwood."

Annemiek wrinkled her nose as she picked up another shoe. A half dozen boxes were lined up next to her, so Kiran was probably in for a good hour of toe shoe percussion before she was satisfied. "We were. But then Sandrine made the mistake of letting our plans slip to her mom."

Kiran chuckled. "Let me guess. Carolee decided your plans were far too casual and started to arrange your schedule down to the minute."

She shook the shoe at him. "If you *ever* tell Carolee that we canceled because of her, I will never forgive you. It's not that I don't love her as much as Sandrine does, but neither one of us wanted this to be an *event*. We just wanted to relax a little before we head to the resort. A little BFF time before the wedding."

"I get it. Carolee can be a bit much."

"She's the very definition of *a bit much*." She paused. "I'm grateful to her, of course, for stepping in when we lost Mom. Dad wasn't the kind of parent to hang around the studio. But Sandrine and I aren't kids anymore, and Sandrine chucked her toe shoes—with enormous relief, I might add—when she decided to go into arts administration. You don't mind, do you, Kir?"

"Mind? Why would I mind a visit from my sister?"

"Oh, I don't know. Because..." She bit her lip. "I might also be hiding from Dad?"

Kiran froze. "Dad's coming here?"

She laughed, light and free. "No, silly. This is the one place he *won't* come." She winced. "Sorry."

"Don't be. It's true." Bernhard Bakker's attitude toward his only son had done a complete one-eighty on the day of the curse. Before, he'd been proud of Kiran—his grades, his early fledging, his family loyalty. But afterward, when Kiran had had to relearn so many large motor skills and the grades were all that was left following what Bernhard viewed as a complete betrayal? He'd transferred all his parental pride to Annemiek.

He edged toward the sofa, cutting a wide berth around Annemiek and her shoe anvil, and sank down on its cushions. "Is he still warning you of the dangers of letting me within a mile of your cake?"

Annemiek snorted. "I don't know why he can't get over that. I certainly did." She poked at the toe of the shoe, a pensive expression on her high-cheekboned face. "You eating my entire cake was less of a disappointment to me than the fact you missed the *Nutcracker* performance."

"I regretted that too. More than anything."

She glanced up at him mischievously. "Because you were sick as a dog?"

"No. Because I wanted to see you dance. I always want to see you dance." Kiran leaned forward, his elbows on his knees. "I hope you know I didn't mean to ruin your birthday."

She'd just lifted another shoe, but she put it down. "You didn't. Dad got me that ice cream cake before anybody even knew the first one was missing." She made a face. "Anyone other than Carolee. I'm not sure why Dad had to share his outrage with her, other than the fact that Mom was inclined to laugh it off."

"She wasn't laughing later."

"No." Annemiek rose gracefully to her feet and hurried over to sit next to Kiran. "Mom never blamed you, you know. All she wanted was for you to get better. To be yourself again."

Kiran smiled wryly. "Too bad that never happened."

"It *did*!" Annemiek said fiercely. "You've always been totally yourself. It's just that your *self* changed, that's all." She kissed his cheek. "But you're still my big brother, and I still love you to pieces."

He wrapped an arm around her shoulders and gave her a squeeze. "Back atcha, princess."

She made a face. "Please. Mom was the princess. I didn't inherit the title."

"Are you sad about that?"

"Are you kidding? Who'd want to get stuck with all that boring royal protocol? I was more than happy to let Auntie Gisela deal with it. I think Mom knew I'd hate it. I've thanked the skies every day that she petitioned to have me removed from the succession before she died." She jiggled his arm. "Want to see my wedding outfit?"

"It's here? Seriously?"

"Where else?" She winked. "It's cake that's your weakness, not finery. Come on."

She tugged him to his feet and towed him down the hall to the guest room, although Kiran made certain that there was a reasonable safety margin between them. She gave him a little shove so that he sat down on the bed with a little bounce, and then swung the closet door open. Hanging on the other side was...a vision.

"Oh, Anni," Kiran breathed. "It's beautiful."

She studied the rainbow-jeweled bodysuit with its flounced overskirt, a smile curving her wide mouth. "I stole the idea from *Crazy Rich Asians*. The actor who played the bride was a ballerina too." She touched the beaded bodice. "Mine isn't quite as jewel-encrusted and the overskirt isn't as elaborate." She ran a finger over the feathers that edged the skirt's top tier. "This is Mom's swan's-down," she said softly.

Kiran's throat tightened and he had to swallow twice before he could speak. "The down she gave you from her last shift?"

Annemiek nodded. "She told me to save it for my wedding. So I did."

"She'd be so happy for you. Just like I am."

She joined him on the bed and laced their fingers together. "Unlike Dad. He's never warmed up to Del."

"Because they're nonbinary?"

"Because he doesn't trust oracles. In a way, I don't blame him. Some oracles are insufferable know-it-alls. But Del's not like that. They're not obnoxious about their visions. They make me feel safe."

Kiran studied their linked hands. "Maybe Dad's still irritated that Del wanted me to have the special dance with you instead of him."

Annemiek snorted, a very un-ballerina-like sound. "Del likes you better. Besides, Dad's annoyed that you're going to be there at all."

They shared a glance and said simultaneously, "Cake."

"Haven't you told Del that story?"

"That happened ages ago. Del said you should partner me in the dance, so I agreed. As an oracle, they may not know *why* something needs to happen, but you can bet that if they say so, it's important."

"What's Del's outfit like?"

She laughed softly. "You know Del. I suggested something like Billy Porter's outfit at the 2019 Oscars."

"The one with the black velvet hoop skirt?"

She nodded. "They'd look fabulous in that, but they're not into ostentation. They're wearing something like Tom Daley's number at the Met Ball." She grinned. "But they got their hair freshly dyed, so it matches the rainbow jewels on my bodysuit."

"Sounds perfect."

She studied her outfit a little dreamily. "Did I ever tell you about the first time we met?"

"I don't think so." Kiran was lying. She had. But he never got tired of hearing it.

"The ballet company was on tour, and we were loading in after a Hunter's Moon concert. I was on my way to the dressing rooms when Del spotted me in the hallway and stopped dead, staring at me as I walked toward them. I asked them if they were all right and they said, 'I'm going to marry you.'" She chuckled. "You should have seen the shock on their face. They told me later it was because nothing *ever* surprises them, but they never saw me coming. It's an oracle thing, apparently. They can't see their own future."

"Then how did they know they were going to marry you?"

She smiled mischievously. "Because they saw mine, of course." Her expression turned solemn. "But seriously, Kir, even though Del thinks you should do that dance, if it worries you or makes you uncomfortable, you don't have to do it."

He met her gaze squarely. "Do *you* want me to do it?" She bit her lip, but then nodded. "Then I will." He forced a smile. "I'm taking lessons, so I've totally got this, sweetie. You don't have to worry about a thing."

I hope.

Taj could almost believe he'd been dropped into a time warp the next day because every minute leading up to Kiran's seven o'clock lesson seemed to last at least a year. With no other students to distract him—nothing but the dwindling balance in his bank account as he paid bills that seemed to breed like rabbit shifters when he wasn't looking—he'd had plenty of time to fantasize about what it would be like.

He'd get to hold Kiran in his arms again. Not super close—this wasn't a *dirty* dancing lesson—but close enough to catch that enticing scent, one that he still hadn't been able to identify. Maybe he could demonstrate a dip. Would a tango be too much? He remembered Kiran's unaccountable clumsiness. *Probably.* Better to keep things simple. However, nobody could blame him for throwing in a couple of flourishes like yesterday's triple spin. The feel of Kiran's body against his own was—

"My, my. You *are* in hot water, aren't you? I didn't think anyone could function with so little money."

Taj jerked at Naberius's smug tone and sent his computer to sleep. "None of your business."

"Well. Not yet." He tapped the monitor with a claw. "But if that balance slides any farther, you'll be in the red and in violation of the relocation requirements. And then, back to Sheol with you, where the hot water is literal, not metaphorical."

"Sheol doesn't have any water."

Naberius shrugged negligently. "Well, lava then."

Taj took a deep breath and spun his chair, putting his desk at his back. The office wasn't as cramped as the closet, but it was still small, and Naberius filled far too much of it. Furthermore, the lobby was visible through a window. If anyone walked in, they couldn't miss Naberius's decidedly non-human bulk. "What do you want? I've got a student arriving in a few minutes, and you can't be here."

"Why not? I've always wanted to watch you work. Although you generally delivered for me—"

"I *always* delivered for you," Taj growled.

"That's still under discussion, now, isn't it? However, I'm curious. I never got to see precisely how you managed to lure my clients to our meetings."

"Lure your victims to their doom, you mean?" Unfortunately, it was never difficult to entice ambitious performers with the promise of fame.

He tutted. "So *gloomy*. They got what they wanted."

"For a price."

"Which was clearly stated." He dusted off his palms in a *clitter* of claws. "Now, about that little task I need you to do for me."

Taj glanced at the clock. Six forty-six. "Could we discuss it later? My student might be early, and if your presence flags me for a Secrecy Pact violation, I'll give you up to the tribunal without a second thought."

"If you're expecting that fellow from last night, the Secrecy Pact is moot."

Taj narrowed his eyes. "Exposing a human to a demon overlord? It's not like the old days, Naberius. Soul negotiations are outlawed, so that loophole is well and truly closed."

"I *mean* that your little morsel isn't human, you idiot."

Taj's jaw dropped. "He's a supe? But…"

Naberius waved a claw at the ceiling. "Turn off your ridiculous lights and you'll see. Honestly, why you want to live with humans *as* a human instead of exploiting them is beyond me."

Before Taj could protest, Naberius vanished with a pop and a whiff of brimstone. Just in time, too, because the subtle door alarm chimed an instant later.

Kiran.

He spotted Taj through the office window and waggled his fingers in a shy wave. Taj stood, sending his wheeled chair careening across the office to bang into the filing cabinet.

"Taj?" Kiran called. "Are you all right?"

"Perfectly fine." Taj tugged his T-shirt straight and exited the office. He didn't have to fake a smile when he spotted Kiran standing inside the door, his elbows tucked tightly to his sides and the bag holding his dance shoes in his hand. Lucifer's balls, but the man was adorable. "My office chair decided it wanted to get better acquainted with the filing cabinet." He hid a wince. Did that sound too supernatural? As if his studio were as enchanted as the *Beauty and the Beast* castle?

Kiran just chuckled, however. "I was afraid my clumsiness might have been contagious, and I wouldn't want that for any dancer." His gaze slid to the poster of his sister and something flitted across his face that Taj couldn't interpret. But at least it wasn't suspicion about animated office furniture.

What am I thinking? If Kiran were as human as Taj believed, his first thoughts wouldn't leap to literal cursed furnishings. He'd assume *metaphor*. Humans didn't realize how many metaphors had their basis in supernatural reality.

On the other hand, if Kiran were a supe as Naberius had claimed... But Kiran hadn't even blinked at the possibility that Taj's chair and filing cabinet were conducting a speed dating encounter. Instead, he'd assumed the more ordinary, the more mundane, the more *human* option: an accident.

Taj kept his smile in place. Naberius was undoubtedly yanking his chain, and Taj refused to fall for it. "Are you ready to get started? You're a bit early, so if you need to take a few minutes to prepare—"

"No! I mean, I'm ready if you are." He glanced around. "Unless you have something else that needs your attention. I always like to leave myself extra time, just in case of, um, unfortunate incidents."

Taj gestured to the Studio B door. "Then let us begin."

As Kiran walked into the dance room—bumping his shoulder against the door frame—Taj studied his rear view, which was far from a hardship. If Kiran *were* a supe, what could he be? Clearly not a vampire, since he'd arrived yesterday in daylight. Not a demon, either, not with a sister whose stellar professional dance career had begun six years ago when she was barely eighteen. No demons had been allowed out of Sheol back then. Probably not fae either, for the same reason. Fae weren't restricted to Faerie the way demons were to Sheol, but they generally chose to live there anyway, to be closer to the One Tree.

Shifter? Maybe a bear? Bears could be clumsy at times, and Kiran had the love handles at his waist that bear shifters tended to develop near the solstice and hibernation season. Granted, it was barely past the autumnal equinox now, but bears started packing on the hibernation pounds in the late fall.

On the other hand, maybe he's just a human who's not obsessed with body image.

And maybe Taj needed to stop ogling those appealing little bulges—perfect handholds for a little enthusiastic sex—and focus on his job.

Teaching Kiran to dance.

Chapter Five

Kiran finished tying his shoes, his fingers only trembling a little. Somehow, in the twenty-four hours since he'd first stepped into Light Fantastic, he'd forgotten how handsome Taj was.

Handsome? He buried a snort. *Talk about understatement.* Taj was stunning. And when he aimed that brilliant smile Kiran's way? *I'll be lucky if my knees don't buckle.* Of course, if they did, he'd be on the floor and out of the danger zone. Or rather, Taj would be out of the danger zone. There wasn't much damage Kiran could do to anyone when he was flat on his ass.

Although if anyone could, it would be me.

He stood up and brushed at his workout pants. "All set."

"Perfect." Taj fiddled with the controls of the sound system on the shelf next to the door and a violin intro wafted out of the speakers in the four corners of the room. "Let's warm up a bit first, shall we?"

With a jolt, Kiran recognized the tune—it was one of Hunter's Moon's hits. But then, the band had human as well as supe fans, so it wasn't *completely* unreasonable. "Do you think that's necessary?"

"Always. We won't be doing anything too strenuous, but we still want our muscles to be warm and supple."

Supple. Why did that word conjure up such erotic visions in Kiran's mind? All the positions that Taj, as a trained dancer, could manage. He forced his mind out of the gutter and tried to follow Taj's movements.

They weren't difficult—knee flexes, ankle rotations, stretches—all of them at the barre so Kiran could hold on with one hand. Since they were stationary exercises, he didn't run into anything either. Maybe this wouldn't be so bad.

"Feeling loose?" Taj asked. When Kiran nodded, he held out his hand. "Let's try some basic steps in the center now."

Kiran clutched the barre harder. "Are you sure? This won't be like *Swing Time*, will it? You won't get fired if you can't teach me to dance?"

"Considering I'm the boss, there's no danger of that." He crooked his fingers. "Come on. You won't hurt me. I promise."

"That's what you think," Kiran muttered, but he took Taj's hand—and nearly dropped it again because of the little *zing* of awareness that zipped up his arm and raised the hairs on the back of his neck. If he didn't have his feet to worry about, he'd have been concerned about body parts a little higher up.

He stumbled slightly, but Taj caught him with effortless strength. "Easy there. I've got you."

"I won't come back with the obvious reply."

Taj raised one eyebrow. "Obvious reply?"

"You know. 'Who's got *you*?'" For some reason, Kiran's feeble joke made Taj tense, and *he* stumbled. "Oh, gods, clumsiness *is* contagious!" He forced himself to take a breath. "Sorry. Overreacting here."

It *wasn't* contagious. It couldn't be. Neither Annemiek nor his mother had been affected, and they'd been closer to him than anybody else in the years since the curse. Besides, the curse wasn't spread through proximity. The conspirators, whoever they were—and a ten-year-old Kiran hadn't been able to identify their whispers, not even the gender of the speakers—had been very clear about that. One had wanted to make absolutely certain that the curse wouldn't spread to anyone nearby, and the other had reassured them: The Tanglefoot curse would only affect the first person to taste the cake.

But Kiran hadn't wanted to take any chances. He'd eaten the whole thing. All of it. Every crumb. Every frosting rosette. And the curse had fallen on him instead.

He hadn't realized at the time that the curse would be permanent. He'd thought it was only for that one show, Annemiek's first *Nutcracker*, the youngest Clara ever at her ballet studio.

He wouldn't have regretted it had the curse ended afterward, but he *really* didn't regret it once he found it was persistent. Because Annemiek deserved her career. And Kiran could live with forever being the clumsy oaf who'd ruined his sister's seventh birthday if it meant she could dance. Kiran's life was full. He was successful. He was well-to-do, as was Annemiek, because what Kiran lacked in large motor skills, he made up for in intelligence and financial savvy. He was occasionally lonely, but wasn't everybody?

"Kiran?"

Kiran looked up from his feet to find Taj peering at him in concern. "Sorry. Did I zone out?"

"For a moment. How about this? Instead of working on anything separately, which you won't need in any case, correct?" Kiran nodded and Taj gifted him with that bone-melting smile and opened his arms. "Shall we dance?"

Kiran hesitated, two decades' worth of his father's disdainful comments playing on an endless loop in his head. Resolutely, he banished them to faint background noise. *This isn't about me. This is about Anni and Del.*

So he stepped forward, into Taj's specific gravity. Holding himself stiff so he wouldn't accidentally carom off Taj's chest, Kiran edged a little closer.

Taj smiled at him, his eyes crinkling at the corners. "Relax. For now, just let me do all the work."

"That would probably be safest for everyone involved, but if you don't mind my saying so, I'll have to at least hold up my end of the deal at the wedding. That means I need to learn how to lead."

"Really?" Taj cocked his head. "Your sister is a dancer. Why not let her lead?"

Kiran blinked. Come to think of it, when he'd seen Annemiek and Del dance together, they switched the lead all the time. It was almost a game with them—stealing the lead, Annemiek told him, which was apparently a thing in ballroom dancing. "That's...actually a good idea." If Annemiek were in charge, there would be fewer opportunities for Kiran to steer her into random furniture or onlookers or—skies forbid—the cake.

Taj clasped Kiran's right hand with his left at about shoulder height. "Good. Now place your left hand on my shoulder, and I'll put my right hand on your..." Taj cleared his throat. "...your waist."

Kiran peered at Taj's face. "Are you okay?"

"Absolutely." Then Taj rested his big, warm hand on Kiran's side, right at the spot where he bulged just a little above his elastic waistband. Kiran's face heated. Taj didn't have an extra ounce on him anywhere. Kiran...did. If Kiran's dad had been here, he'd have made some disparaging remark about Kiran's need to cut back on sweets. But Taj didn't say a thing.

Why would he? I'm a temporary student. Still, it was refreshing not to have someone passing silent judgment on him about his body. In fact, the expression on Taj's face was almost...reverent. As though he *liked* touching Kiran. As though Kiran *deserved* such admiration, such care.

"We're going to do a simple box step now. I'm going to hold you a little closer so I can position your legs with mine. Is that okay?"

Kiran nodded. "Absolutely." *More than.* The last time he'd been snugged up against Taj's chest and twirled across the floor, he'd felt weightless. Capable. Graceful. All the things that had seemed outside his reach since the curse.

This time was no different. Taj's slight pressure against his lower back, the strength of his leg slotted between Kiran's, put Kiran's foot in exactly the right place, precisely on the beat of the music. Another step, and he was grinning. A third and he was laughing.

A fourth and he was flying.

Taj's smile sent his stomach into a loop-the-loop. "See? You can do it."

"I'm pretty sure you're the one doing it, but I'll take the compliment."

"Excellent. Now, hold on. We're going to do a turn. You don't get dizzy, do you?"

Other than dizzy over Taj's body pressed so close to his, Taj's gorgeous face inches away, Taj's delicious subtly smoky scent surrounding him? "Not a bit."

"Here we go."

And they did. Once, twice, three times, and Kiran had never felt anything as thrilling since the first time he'd lifted off the lake when he fledged. He caught his breath, as if that would let him hold on to the feeling for a few seconds longer.

Annemiek always said that she never found being partnered in any pas de deux at all romantic. But for her, dance was work, her partners the other people in the company whom she knew all too well—and more often than not found annoying.

Maybe that's why this felt so momentous to Kiran. Because he'd never danced before. Or at least not for years and never with a partner.

However, he doubted whether the fizz Taj stirred in his blood would fade, even if they danced every day forever.

"Ready for the dip?" Taj asked.

"Dip?" Kiran had claimed he wouldn't get dizzy. He'd lied. "Can't we turn again?"

Taj chuckled. "That's the lead-in. Two turns and then the dip." Another gentle pressure on his back and Kiran magically knew how to step back and to the side.

"How do you do that?"

"Do what?"

"Send me in the right direction with just a couple of touches and a weight shift?"

"Ah, that's partnering for you, my friend." Taj grinned. "That's dancing." They spun once, twice, and then suddenly Kiran was bent backward over Taj's arm, looking up at him as he was suspended in Taj's confident hold. "It's magic."

"Yes," Kiran said breathlessly. "It is."

And because Taj was hovering over him with those bedroom eyes, Kiran did the unthinkable: He stretched up and kissed Taj's full lips.

And promptly fell on his ass.

"I'm sorry. I'm sorry." He scrambled up, slipping once and banging his knee on the floor. "I didn't mean to... I shouldn't..."

"Kiran, wait."

Kiran didn't. He managed to stumble out of the dance room and down the hall to the men's room, only running into the wall twice. The room had lockers and benches in the rear and sinks and toilet stalls near the door. Kiran glanced around wildly, but there was no other exit.

Jeez, if I wanted to escape, I shouldn't have backed myself into a literal corner.

But then Taj was looming in the doorway. "Kiran."

Kiran hid his eyes behind his hands. "I'm so sorry. I shouldn't have done that without asking permission. No. Strike that. I shouldn't have done it at all. You're my instructor. This is your place of business. You don't want random students flinging themselves at you."

"You're right on all counts," Taj said, and Kiran wished *very* hard for a pit to open under his feet and drop him straight to Sheol. "Except you're not a random student."

Kiran peeked from behind his fingers. "I'm not?"

Taj shook his head, smiling ruefully. "You're my first student. Currently my *only* student. Consequently, there are many reasons why I shouldn't do this." He approached Kiran slowly, every movement graceful and—*gah!*—supple. He gently took Kiran's hands away from his face. "And only one why I should."

"Do what?"

"Kiss you."

Kiran swallowed, his mouth gone dry. "Wh-what's the reason?"

"Because you want it. And because I want it too. More than anything that I've wanted for a long, long time."

And Taj cradled Kiran's face and kissed him.

Bad idea. Bad idea. Such a bad idea.

But with Kiran's lips so soft under his, Taj didn't care.

Kiran was absolutely right: Yes, this was Taj's place of business; yes, Kiran was his student—at least for the remainder of this lesson and two more; and, yes, maintaining a professional distance was critical.

But Taj hadn't had a man in his arms who *wanted* to be there since he was manifested, and it was *glorious.*

Kiran's taste as their tongues touched and retreated and surged and stroked was as intoxicating as the finest wine, although as fresh and cool as a mountain stream. It was nothing short of a revelation.

Taj's role as a minion had never included sexual seduction—he wasn't an incubus, and Naberius's targets had been more interested in the adulation of crowds than the love of one particular person. Had sex been involved a time or two? Yes. But only as a means to Naberius's end.

Transactional, with Taj always so focused on tracking the unfamiliar choreography that he hadn't had time to enjoy the experience.

Not that he could have, anyway. *Enjoyment* wasn't something Naberius had been concerned with, at least not for Taj, nor for any of his targets.

So this...this tidal wave of joy that threatened to drown him, the tingle in his fingers, the fire in his belly—and below—those were all new, all thrilling.

All Kiran.

When Kiran's arms came around Taj's back, Taj moaned —something he'd never done before, but it just felt so *good*, so *right*. Kiran's sturdy body was cooler than Taj's demon heat, a fever balm that soothed at the same time it inflamed. Kiran's erection, though, hard against Taj's own cock? *That* wasn't cool. That was as white hot as the fire in Taj's blood.

How can I let this go? He would have to, though. Kiran was human, and humans were off-limits to demons now.

Wait. Although Taj's brain was scrambled by the way Kiran's palms skated across his back to rest at his waist, Naberius's snide remark insinuated itself into his consciousness: *"Turn off your ridiculous lights and you'll see."*

Taj tightened his arms around Kiran as, with a thought, he flicked off the dressing room lights.

Kiran, his eyes closed, was nuzzling Taj's throat, nipping the skin playfully. "You taste so good. Salty and sweet and rich, like salted caramel." He opened his eyes and blinked as if trying to clear his sight. "Taj...it's dark."

"Don't worry. The lights are on a motion sensor." He kissed Kiran's forehead, his cheekbone, his lips. "Guess these particular motions weren't registering. Afraid you'll lose me in the dark?"

Kiran chuckled. "I think I could find you even in someplace as lightless as Sheol." When Taj froze, Kiran squinted up at him, concern on his face—which Taj could see perfectly well with his Sheol-adapted sight. "Taj? Is something wrong?"

"Not a thing," Taj breathed. Because now, with the special neutralizing lights gone, that Sheol-adapted sight could see something else: Kiran's aura.

He really is a supe. Based on the feathery, gold-tinged blue that surrounded him, so bright Taj had to squint, he must be a swan shifter. No wonder Annemiek was such a fabulous dancer—she was a swan, too.

Although why Kiran should be so clumsy was a mystery. Some issue with his *calon,* the special organ that every supe had, that, according to their nature, activated their special abilities? Taj was about to look more closely when the muffled sound of "Song of the Volga Boatmen" wafted into the room.

"Oh, gods," Kiran muttered, "that's my father." He smiled up at Taj in the dark. "I have to answer. It might be something about the wedding, and he's impossible to reach."

Taj captured his face for one more lingering kiss as the music cut off and then started again immediately. "Then you'd better get it."

Kiran peered around. "Guess I should wave my arms or something to get the lights to come back on. You don't want to know the damage I could do trying to navigate an unfamiliar landscape in the dark."

"As to that..." Taj snapped his fingers and mentally flicked the lights back on. "Mission accomplished."

Kiran's brilliant grin caught Taj right below his heart. "Thank you."

As Kiran started to move past him—bumping his shin against the benches that fronted the locker banks—Taj caught his hand. "Kiran. There's something I want to say to you. To tell you."

The song cut off and started again. Was it Taj's imagination that it sounded *angry*? Then again, that song never sounded exactly cheerful. Chances were good that Kiran and his father had a difficult relationship.

"I'm sorry," Kiran said, rising on his toes to kiss Taj softly. "Hold that thought and we'll talk after I get Dad sorted."

He hurried out of the room, bumping his shoulder on the door frame.

"Well. *That* was entertaining."

Taj whirled to find Naberius stretched out along one bench, ankles crossed. "What are you doing here?"

A pout looked very odd on a foot-long beak, but somehow Naberius managed. "Is that any way to greet your own dear father?"

"You're not my *father*," Taj growled. "You're my *progenitor*. That's all."

Naberius flicked his claws. "Semantics." He swung his hooves to the floor and sat up. "I'm here to discuss your next job, of course."

"I don't work for you anymore."

"Ah, but you *did*, didn't you? So many dreams realized and crushed through the ages. Really, it was gratifying."

"Their dreams were only crushed because you called in their soul markers at the height of their fame."

"Yes, but they *knew* that would happen. It was right there in the fine print under Clause XIV." He sniffed. "Not my fault if they didn't read it."

"You—"

"That's not the point. Most of my...clients were interested in improving their own fortunes. All but one."

Taj crossed his arms. "Let me guess. That's the one that's still outstanding."

Naberius scowled. "Yes, drat the luck. If it was anybody whining about their own situation, I could ignore it and point to Clause XIV. But this one negotiated for somebody else's benefit. I suppose you could call it selfless." Naberius spit out the word as if it tasted as bitter as shame. "So I'm bound to deliver."

That was one of the few restrictions on demons engaged in soul-collecting. The contract was sacrosanct in Sheol: The demon had to deliver the goods just as inevitably as the victim had to surrender to their eventual fate.

"What does that have to do with me?"

Naberius grinned, and a beak with teeth *that* long was just wrong, although Taj had gotten used to it over the eons. That grin appeared whenever Naberius was about to close a deal. "Why, because you're the one who screwed up, of course."

For an instant, unfamiliar ice crusted Taj's heart. "I never screwed up unless you ordered me to." Skipping rehearsals, missing call times, bobbling auditions—Taj had done them all to make way for Naberius's *clients*.

"Not precisely." He waggled a claw in front of Taj's face. "You delivered the curse, but you didn't remain to see it executed properly."

"Curse?" Taj frowned. "You mean this so-called selfless act involved injuring somebody else? Somebody who wasn't contracted? That's a violation of terms too."

"Oh, pooh. Every contract that involves elevating one person presupposes that somebody else will be the lesser for it. This was just more...direct. Besides, the curse wasn't for her own benefit. It was on behalf of her daughter. The curse was directed at her daughter's rival, and it wasn't *lethal*. Just...a change in circumstances."

Taj snorted. "Right. I'm guessing that change wasn't exactly a dream for the triangulated victim."

"We'll never know because it misfired."

"You mean you actually cast a curse that failed?" Taj chortled. "So much for your claim of 100% success."

Naberius glared, his eyes behind those stupid goggles glowing red. "I didn't say the curse *failed*. I said it *misfired*. It was extremely effective, simply on the wrong person."

Taj glanced toward the door. With his demon-enhanced hearing—something Naberius had insisted on, the better for Taj to overhear rumors and secrets—he could hear Kiran murmuring into his phone, his tone terse. "Stop dancing around the issue and spit it out. Kiran could come back any minute and you"—he jabbed a finger at Naberius—"cannot be here."

"Think back about twenty years, give or take. Do you recall delivering a ballerina birthday cake to a house not so far from here while I completed negotiations with my client in the next room?"

Taj didn't have to think very hard. He'd wondered at that entire situation. Naberius's targets had always been adults in the performing arts, since those were the people he envied. Taj had assumed the client must have some relationship to dance, given the beautifully decorated cake, but... "You cursed a *child*?"

"I cursed the *cake*. A perfectly crafted Tanglefoot curse, if I do say so myself. The client was the one who targeted the kid."

"Hairsplitting, you asshole. You had to know what she planned. You'd have spelled it out in the contract. Explicitly."

He waved away Taj's anger as though it were no more annoying than a dust mote. "Irrelevant since the curse misfired. It didn't land on the client's target because somebody else took that first all-important bite. In fact, he took *all* the bites, because *you* didn't remain to guard the cake."

"Since when did I ever guard birthday cakes?"

He lifted his chin, wattles wobbling. "You should have known."

"I never knew the details of your deals. You made sure of that so I couldn't do an end run around you and warn the victim."

"*Clients.* Not victims. *Clients.* In any case, it's time to make things right."

"No." Taj planted his feet wide and crossed his arms. "I'm not going to be a part of injuring a child, no matter what you say."

"She's not a child anymore, you fool. She's an adult."

"So? She still doesn't owe you anything." He thought of Kiran, so earnest and unselfish and *tasty*, mere steps away.

Now that Taj knew the truth of his nature, he planned to confess. To tell Kiran the truth about himself and see if they could make something of this attraction. He'd waited long enough. Wasn't he due to have one of *his* dreams come true for a change?

"I know what you're thinking," Naberius sing-songed. "But before you get on your high horse and imagine a little rose-covered cottage somewhere for you and your swan shifter, imagine *this*: What will he do, how far will he kick your ass with those incredibly clumsy feet, when he finds out that *you* were the one who delivered that cursed cake to his sister?"

Taj's hands went numb and his arms fell to his sides. "The curse was intended for *Annemiek Bakker*?"

"Indeed. And the only reason it didn't land was because..." Naberius let the word linger in the air. "...her older brother ate the entire cake first."

Chapter Six

Kiran glanced at the dance room door, aching in more ways than one to return to the dressing room, to Taj's arms. Figures that his father would call him—multiple times—and then, as soon as he answered, put him on hold.

Gods, Taj had kissed him. Okay, so he'd kissed Taj first, but Taj had kissed back, and it was pretty obvious that Kiran didn't *disgust* him, not with the ridge of Taj's cock snugged up hard and hot against his own.

If he could just get his father off the phone, he could go back. Kiss some more. *Feel* some more. But Kiran shied away from doing anything other than that. Not here. Not in Taj's place of business, because having sex somewhere kids would eventually be hanging out was just too squicky.

Maybe Taj would agree to come home with— No, that wouldn't work. Not now, anyway, not with Annemiek in the guest room and the wedding only days away. But afterward? Yes, that could work.

When Kiran got back from Wildwood on Sunday night, he'd call Taj. Set up an actual date. Invite him up to the condo, because when it came to dates, it was far easier for Kiran to manage without accidents if he was in an environment he could control, like his own kitchen and living room.

His own bedroom.

Too fast. Too soon. He didn't want to appear overly eager. He'd heard that turned some men off. On the other hand, Taj didn't *seem* turned off—quite the opposite—so maybe he felt the same kind of instant spark that Kiran had. If Taj had been a supe, Kiran would have staked half his Q1 profits—and Q1 had been *really* good—that they'd had a *calon*-to-*calon* connection, the kind only true soulmates could have.

But Taj was human. So that wasn't possible.

But maybe we could have a relationship, anyway. It wasn't as if Kiran lived a particularly supernatural lifestyle. Since he couldn't fly and didn't live near a lake, he didn't shift often. Could he live the rest of his life hiding that part of himself from a partner, a lover, a...husband?

Whoa, there. Getting way *ahead of myself.*

They'd had one make-out session and already Kiran was picking out curtains. He needed to get a grip. He needed—

"Kiran," his father said, his voice terse, at once both long-suffering and impatient. "I'm at City Hall. Meet me at the PacWest Starbucks in ten minutes."

Kiran huffed an exasperated sigh. Trust his father to make unreasonable demands. "Sorry, Dad. Not possible."

"Don't be ridiculous. You needn't wait for a train. Call for a car."

"I'm not at home right now, and I'm rather busy."

There was a brief silence on the line. "What do you mean, you're not at home? You're always at home."

"I'm *often* at home, because that's where I work as well as live. But I go to other places as well. I'll be going to another place this weekend, if you recall."

"That's what I want to talk to you about." His father hummed under his breath, a sure sign he was leading up to something Kiran didn't want to hear. "You need to contact your sister and tell her you can't come to the wedding."

Kiran's jaw sagged. He held the phone away from his ear and actually stared at the screen, even though he couldn't see anything but his wallpaper. He'd started refusing video calls almost as soon as they'd become common, so he wouldn't have to see that disappointed expression on his father's face every time they spoke.

Which, granted, wasn't often. But even once a month was more than enough.

"Why in all the hells would I do that?"

"I shouldn't have to tell you."

Kiran leaned against the wall, his back tense, even though he wanted nothing more than to pace. "I'm afraid you'll have to say it. I'm not about to do your work for you."

His father grunted. "That's you all over. You never change. You never think of anyone other than yourself."

"On the contrary, I'm thinking of Annemiek and Del. Anni asked me to be an attendant. Del asked me to partner her in the before-dinner dance."

"Your sister is too tender-hearted, and Delta... Well, oracles are capricious at the best of times. Delta holds a grudge against me for forbidding the marriage."

"Yeah, that might do it," Kiran said dryly. "Particularly since you have no power whatsoever over Anni's life or decisions."

"I'm her *father*."

Kiran forbore from saying, "You're my father too." It wouldn't have helped, anyway. Bernhard Bakker preferred to distance himself from his oldest child whenever possible.

"If you disagreed with Anni's choices, you should have mentioned them to her early enough for her to do something about it without disarranging her entire wedding."

"I *tried*. She wouldn't *listen*. She could be a princess. Her mother's bloodline entitled her. She didn't have to settle for—"

"Stop. Right. There. Anni didn't *settle*. She fell in love. And she's never wanted to be a princess. So give it up, Dad. It's never happening."

Kiran could imagine his father fuming. It wasn't hard. He'd seen enough of that over the years. It took a good two minutes before he said, "Fine. But at least talk her into letting me partner her in the pre-dinner dance. It can't matter to Delta. I'm only thinking of you, Kiran."

Oh, really? "I find that hard to believe."

"Do you *want* to display your...your awkwardness in front of all the wedding guests? Do you really want everyone whispering about you, laughing at you, *embarrassed* by you when they ought to be celebrating Annemiek and Delta?"

Kiran winced. Trust his father to hit on exactly the issue that worried Kiran most. Not because he cared what other people said about him, but because it might pull the focus from where it truly belonged—with the newlyweds.

"I'm working on that, Dad. Anni and I have discussed it, and she's certain." Although three lessons were probably not enough. *I need magical shoes like Taj's.*

"And she's also certain she'll trust you that close to cake?"

Kiran ground his teeth at his father's suspicious tone. "You really need to get over that. I was ten years old, Dad." He glanced at the door again. Taj could come in at any moment. In fact, Kiran was surprised he hadn't already shown up. Thanks to his father, though, Kiran had completely lost the mood—for either an extended make-out session or to continue the dance lesson.

"Now, about the wedding gift. Do you need money? You can't stint on it. A paltry gift will reflect poorly on our family."

"I don't need your money, Dad. I've got plenty of my own."

"Kiran." His father managed to sound both patronizing and accusatory. Quite a feat. "You needn't pretend with me. You're unemployed."

"I'm *self-employed*, Dad. It's not the same. And for your information, my gift to Anni and Del is their honeymoon trip. I'm sending them to a seaside villa in Corfu for three weeks. Private beach. Personal chef. Chauffeur. Maid service."

"Wha—"

"Already paid for. *In cash.* Now excuse me. I've got things to do." He disconnected the call before his father could get another word in.

"Kiran?" Taj said softly from the doorway. His worried frown didn't make him look any less handsome. "Is everything okay?"

Kiran took a deep breath and forced a smile. "Yes. Of course. But I'm afraid I'll have to cut our...lesson short." He tried to push his father's warnings out of his head. "Oh. You said there was something you wanted to tell me?"

Taj's smile was strained. "It was nothing. You're not leaving because I... Because we..."

"No! Gods, no." Kiran hurried across the room and stumbled at the perfect spot to fall into Taj's arms. *Score one for clumsiness.* He hugged Taj tight, and although Taj merely rested his hands at Kiran's waist instead of returning the hug, he kissed the top of Kiran's head. "But I do have to go. I'll see you tomorrow? Same time?"

Taj nodded. "Same time."

He watched as Kiran changed back into his street shoes. Kiran couldn't quite interpret the expression on his face. When Kiran left the studio, Taj raised his hand in farewell, and his smile was almost sad.

Kiran promised himself he'd explain to Taj later. Next week. *After I've completely sabotaged Anni's wedding.*

He tried to tell himself that his crisis of confidence was only the result of his father's call. But more than anything, he wanted Annemiek and Del to have a perfect day. He should have known better. Three dance lessons weren't enough to make him perfect or even marginally competent. He snorted as he got off the MAX train and trudged toward his building. *For that, I'd need* truly *magical shoes.*

He froze in front of the New Age store, causing a pedestrian behind him to bump into *him* for once. *Could he get magical shoes?* This store was owned by a witches' collective. *Could they bespell his dance shoes for him?*

He immediately rejected that idea. Witches were all about natural consequences. They'd consider his inability to dance to be the natural consequence of eating that cursed cake—not that he'd tell them about that. He'd never told anybody about the curse, not even Annemiek.

But there were other, more...off-the-grid magical practitioners. If he could find one of them...

He slipped into the store's vestibule and studied their bulletin board. Most of the flyers were innocuous enough, keyed to the human New Age crowd who were less likely to question extra-normal experiences. But half-hidden behind a poster for a "What Color Is Your Chakra?" seminar was a tattered flyer, produced on a printer that obviously needed a new toner cartridge:

Looking for something special? That one-of-a-kind artifact? Call Ronnie. He delivers.

Half the phone number flags at the bottom of the sheet had been removed. With a glance over his shoulder, Kiran tore one off and tucked it into his pocket.

Annemiek and Del would have their perfect wedding, damn it. No matter what Kiran had to pay to make it happen.

If Taj had been nervous about Kiran's arrival yesterday, it was nothing compared to today. His desires warred with his conscience, because no matter how attracted he was to Kiran, how much he longed to have him in his arms again, to kiss him again, to feel him again, no matter how certain he was that Kiran was a perfect fit for him, he couldn't let things go farther until Kiran knew the truth: Not only was Taj a supe, a demon, but he was also the one responsible for Kiran's large motor skill challenges.

Because regardless of what he said to Naberius, Taj knew it really was his fault. If he'd stayed to make sure the curse was delivered properly, it wouldn't have landed on Kiran.

No, it would have landed on Annemiek.

And *that* was just as unconscionable. If Taj had known what the plan was, that the cake had been cursed, had been intended for a *child*, would he have risked refusing Naberius's orders? He never had before that and certainly hadn't afterward. His only act of overt rebellion had been choosing to come here to the Upper World and try to make his way among humans *as* a human, with his demon abilities neutralized by the spells in the studio and in the glasses he wore when he ventured outside.

There was a reason he'd named his studio Light Fantastic: It was the lights that made him a part of this world, the lights that gave him a future.

Or would if he could manage to attract enough business to pay his way.

He couldn't decide what was right. He *could* keep his mouth shut, finish Kiran's last two lessons, and let him walk out the door for good.

When he thought about that, though, his heart—that suddenly resurrected cinder—squeezed so hard he nearly doubled over in phantom pain.

But I can't be with him unless I come clean. About all of it.

And if he did that, Kiran would probably walk away on his own.

Talk about a lose-lose situation.

Taj sighed and did what he always did when he had a decision to make.

He danced.

With his playlist on shuffle, he let his body move across the floor—leaps, spins, intricate footwork. When the intro to "There's Got to be Something Better Than This" played right after his last pose in "Dancing Through Life," he nearly snorted. But then Ben Taylor's cover of "I Try" started next, and that was a little too much, even for Taj. The lyrics echoed his own inner struggle, and he couldn't. He just couldn't. He braced his hands on the wall over the ballet barre, chest heaving.

"Don't stop."

Kiran's soft words brought Taj's head up with a snap, but he didn't turn. How could he face Kiran, knowing what he knew now? What Kiran *didn't* know?

"I'm sorry," he croaked. "I lost track of time."

"Don't be sorry." Kiran's footsteps, with their interrupted cadence—*he stumbles because of me*—approached across the floor. "You're beautiful when you dance." He chuckled, a little breathlessly. "Well, you're beautiful when you're not dancing, so no surprise there."

Taj made himself turn around and gaze down into those soft gray eyes. "Thank you. But I should have been ready for you. For your lesson, I mean. I must be all sweaty and —"

Kiran put a finger across Taj's lips and Taj's eyes fluttered closed at the touch. "You're not sweaty at all. Only your usual glow."

"Glow. Right." That was the best Naberius could manage in Taj's manifestation matrix: Demons didn't sweat, but to make Taj fit in with the physically intense performing arts world, he had to make him at least appear to exert himself. "I'll change my shirt while you put on your dance shoes and we'll—"

"No."

Taj blinked. "No?"

"No." Kiran took a deep breath. "I'm paying for the lesson time, right?"

"Yeeesss," Taj said slowly.

"Then, for this lesson, I want you to dance. *For* me, not *with* me. I want to watch you, Taj." Kiran's smile was crooked, wistful. "You said that the purpose of dance was to bring joy. I want to see *your* joy. Please?"

Taj's heart threatened to bound out of his chest. Nobody had ever wanted to simply watch him for pleasure before. When he was Naberius's minion, auditioning for shows to get close to the chosen *clients*, the directors were simply judging him for his suitability for their shows. Of course, since one of Taj's abilities was to appear precisely suitable for any show, he always got cast unless the purpose of auditioning was *not* to get cast in order for the chosen target to win the role instead.

As for the targets themselves, they only watched Taj to detect weaknesses, to look for ways to outshine him. Little did they know they didn't have to do anything but sell their soul.

So he smiled down at Kiran. "All right. For you."

He moved to the sound system—making sure to remove "I Try" from the playlist—and he danced. For Kiran. For himself.

For joy.

Kiran's gaze burned like ice and fire along his skin, never wavering, although there was something in Kiran's rapt expression, something almost painful, as if he were gazing through a window at something he could never have.

Taj could recognize that expression, because every time he caught sight of himself in the mirror, he wore exactly the same one.

When the music finally came to an end on the last notes of "Bridge Over Troubled Water," Taj held his last pose for an instant longer, breathing hard the way he'd learned to do over the years so he could blend in with the human dancers. He glanced at the clock. Nearly eight. Their time was almost up.

But Taj was the boss, wasn't he? Who said he couldn't extend their time? It wasn't as though anybody else was beating down the door, clamoring for his services. He lowered his arms and turned with what he hoped was a seductive smile on his lips.

However, it died at the expression on Kiran's face. That painful yearning was back. Yearning Taj could handle—he was buried under a boatload of it himself—but the pain? He'd do anything, give anything to take away Kiran's pain, whatever it was. But he didn't know how, so he just stood there with his arms hanging limp at his sides.

Kiran rose and walked toward Taj, carefully placing one foot in front of the other. He made it all the way without a single stumble or misstep and placed his hands on Taj's chest. "Thank you. That was wonderful. *You're* wonderful."

Taj covered Kiran's hands with his own. "You're the one who's wonderful. Extraordinary."

Kiran laughed deprecatingly. "Me? The only non-ordinary thing about me is my extraordinary clumsiness. But I appreciate the sentiment."

Taj took his courage in both hands. "Will you stay? We can still have your lesson. We don't have to count the last hour against your time."

Kiran shook his head. "No. That wouldn't be fair. And I, um, have another appointment." He glanced at the clock. "In fact, I need to hurry if I don't want to be late. But thank you again." He kissed Taj softly, chastely. "I couldn't have asked for anything better than that." And he winked.

Taj laughed in spite of himself. "Did you just throw a lyric at me?"

"Not a lyric so much as a song title, but Taj..." He rested his palm lightly against Taj's cheek. "You really are wonderful."

Taj dropped his chin. *I should tell him. I should tell him everything right now.* It wasn't fair for Kiran to believe Taj was more than he was, more admirable than he was. "I—"

"Yikes! The time!" Kiran stumbled back and Taj caught his hand to steady him before he fell. "I really do have to leave."

"I'll walk you out." Taj kept Kiran's hand in his and Kiran didn't trip or stumble or bump into anything even once all the way to the door. Because as Naberius's minion at the time of the curse, Taj could neutralize it as long as they were in contact.

At least I can give him that.

Chapter Seven

Kiran refused to look back after he walked out of the studio because he was afraid that if Taj still wore that unhappy expression, he wouldn't be able to leave at all. He didn't risk taking the train downtown to the Bullpen, the Portland shifter bar. He called for an Uber instead and tipped the driver extra for not laughing when Kiran nearly tripped over the curb when he got out of the car.

On the surface, the Bullpen didn't look any different from any other storefront, but its door spells ensured that only supes could enter. Humans didn't even notice it, or else had their attention caught by the bar farther down the street.

Kiran slipped through the door without incident— maybe the door spells prevented people from running into them too—and peered around in the dimness. He'd never been inside before. Because of his curse, he preferred to avoid crowded places, and from all he'd heard, the Bullpen was always bustling, especially on nights when the fight pens in its subbasement were in use.

Kiran shivered. Supe against supe in shifted form. Not something he'd ever consider, even though swans were fiercer than most people imagined.

The bartender behind the U-shaped bar gave Kiran a nod, probably noting his aura to make sure he belonged, door spells notwithstanding. Most of the tables were full, the din of so many people in such a relatively small space speaking at the top of their voices almost overwhelming.

Kiran winced, but set his jaw. *All the better for not being overheard.*

He scanned the room until he spotted a slight man with a thin, clever face sitting alone at a two-top in the far corner. The man raised a tentative hand, although it wasn't really necessary. Kiran was there to meet Ronnie Purl, ferret shifter, and he'd never seen anybody whose vibe screamed *ferret* more than the man in the corner.

He would *be sitting where I have to navigate the entire room to get to him.*

To avoid the busy servers and the patrons walking between tables, Kiran skirted the edge of the room, one hand on the wall whenever possible. He arrived at the table without incident—mostly.

"Ronnie?" he asked.

"The same." Ronnie gestured to the chair across from him. "Take a load off."

Kiran eyed the chair. Sitting with his back to the bar ruffled his feathers, so he scooted it to the side, which gave him at least a peripheral view of the room. "Can I buy you a drink?"

Ronnie lifted his half-empty beer mug. "Nah. I'm fixed."

Kiran licked his dry lips. "You have...them?"

Ronnie grinned, exposing sharp, slightly yellowed incisors. "Right here." He patted a leather satchel next to his chair. "Want to take a look?"

"In here?" Kiran squeaked. "I thought we'd go…"

"Where? A back alley somewhere? They're shoes, dude, not porn or heroin." He puffed out his chest. "And I wouldn't peddle those, anyway. I'm a respectable businessman." He scrunched up his face. "Well, a businessman anyway." He jerked his finger at the ceiling. "You know nothing illegal can happen in here. The spells prevent it."

"Of course. Sorry." Kiran wiped his damp palms on his trousers. "Then yes, I'd like to see them."

Ronnie unbuckled the flap on the satchel and flipped it up to display…

"They're red."

"So?"

"I can't wear *red* shoes. Don't you have anything in black?"

"Look, pal. These things don't grow on trees. You want magic shoes? This is all I got."

"They'll make me dance well?"

"Guaranteed." Ronnie placed a hand on his chest. "100%."

Kiran reached for them.

"Oi! What are you doing?"

"I need to try them on. If they don't fit—"

"They'll fit. That's part of the magic. But you can't put them on. They're a onetime thing. You can only use them once, so save 'em for when you need 'em."

Kiran narrowed his eyes. "How can I be sure they'll work, then? These aren't coming cheap. What if I pay you and just end up with an ordinary pair of shoes?" He glanced down at the bag again. "Well, ordinary other than being *red*."

"You need to get over that. The spell's legit or your money back."

"Uh huh. Sure."

Ronnie widened his eyes in a failed attempt to look innocent. "Cross my heart. Your payment won't clear until after the spell's activated. You saw to that." He scowled then. "Although I'm hurt that you don't trust me enough to not put strings on my money."

"I'm a businessman, too, Ronnie. A financial manager. And I didn't get where I am—or get my clients where *they* are—through blind trust. But don't feel slighted. When it comes to money, love, and power, I don't give anyone a free pass."

"Fine. But you won't be needing the failsafe. My goods are first-rate. Top shelf. Nothing sketchy." He glanced around furtively. "At all. Now, have we got a deal?"

Kiran peered down at the shoes' heels. "Are they red all over?"

"Dude," Ronnie said, warning in his tone.

"Sorry." What choice did Kiran have? No matter how good a teacher Taj was or how wonderful Kiran felt in his arms, he wasn't dancing with Taj in three days. He was dancing with Annemiek, and he needed all the help he could get. So he nodded. "We have a deal."

Ronnie grinned again. "You won't be sorry." He pulled the latest model iPhone out of his pocket—Kiran noted that Ronnie's screen was intact, unlike his own—and pulled up the contract he'd texted Kiran a copy of last night. "Just sign here."

Kiran swiped his signature with a finger and the screen flared green—as did the shoes. He glanced down at them in alarm. Red shoes were bad enough, but chartreuse? The glow faded, though, leaving the shoes their previous vivid scarlet.

"There you go. Spell's keyed to you now." Ronnie re-buckled the flap and handed the satchel to Kiran. "Bag's included at no extra charge."

"Th-thanks." He set it gingerly in his lap and eyed his escape route. Maybe he could pick up some black shoe polish on the way home. Shoe dye? Was that a thing? Would it work on bespelled shoes?

"Oh. One other thing," Ronnie said, placing a hand on the bag. "Now that you're keyed to the spell, you can't dance until you put the shoes on."

No dancing? No chance to twirl in Taj's arms again? Kiran's belly sank. "Why not?"

"How should I know? I don't make this stuff. I just..." There was that furtive glance again.

"You just what?"

Ronnie made an expansive gesture. "Handle the supply chain."

Kiran sighed. "Any other instructions I should know about?"

"Don't think so." Ronnie pulled a creased, dog-eared piece of parchment out of his fleece vest pocket. The lower left corner was torn off. "Nah. Nothing on here. Paper's mostly blank." He screwed up his face, squinting at the ceiling. "Fellow who sold it to me said something... What was it?" He sucked his upper lip between his teeth. "Nah. It's gone. Couldn't have been important though, or I'd have remembered." He tapped his temple and winked. "Mind like a steel trap. That's me."

"Uh huh."

Ronnie held out a hand for Kiran to shake. "Pleasure doing business with you." He pushed out of his chair. "Now if you'll excuse me, I've got to see a man about a horse." With his beer mug in one hand, he strolled over the bar and perched on a stool.

"Shoe polish," Kiran muttered. "Lots and lots of shoe polish is in my future."

Shoe polish and an apologetic call to Taj, canceling his last lesson. He sighed. It was just as well. He was getting far too attached, and supe/human couplings weren't simply frowned on from the perspective of the Secrecy Pact.

Except for the special cases that lobbyists had gotten grandfathered in—and hapless swan shifters didn't qualify under any of those—they were forbidden.

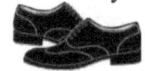

Taj didn't even flinch when Naberius materialized, legs crossed tailor-fashion, on top of Taj's file cabinet at six forty-five. "What do you want now?"

"Is that any way to greet someone who has only your best interests at heart?" His crest drooped, but Taj wasn't fooled. Even if he hadn't had centuries of gauging Naberius's moods, he'd seen those TikTok videos. Despite Naberius's ego-driven delusions about his own talent, he just wasn't that good an actor.

"The day you have anyone's best interests at heart other than your own is the day a Ben and Jerry's opens next to the lava river in Sheol. Come on. Let's have it."

Naberius unfolded his legs and let them dangle over the edge of the file cabinet, drumming his hooves against the metal drawers. "This." He reached into a *nothingness* and pulled out...

"Is that a wedding cake topper?"

"It is." He studied it, his head cocked. "A lovely bit of craftsmanship, if I do say so myself."

Taj pointed at the miniature figures. "The one on the right is a dead ringer for Annemiek Bakker. Please tell me you're not trying to curse her *wedding cake* since you failed miserably with her seventh birthday cake."

Naberius stuck his beak in the air. "*I* didn't fail. My curse was perfect, as you ought to know, since you've seen the evidence of it with your own eyes. Your little bit on the side—"

Taj surged out of his chair. "*Don't* talk about him like that."

"My, my, my," Naberius purred. "Isn't *this* interesting? After all these years, I do believe my esteemed minion has developed *feelings*."

Taj plopped back in his chair. "There are several things wrong with that statement. First, I'm not your minion anymore. Second, even when I was, you never *esteemed* me."

"Don't stop now. Surely you've got a third grievance just begging to be let out."

Taj crossed his arms and fixed his gaze firmly on the copy machine. "I always had feelings," he muttered. *I just couldn't do anything about them.*

Naberius crowed—actually crowed, like a rooster at dawn. "I could have done so much with that knowledge back in the day. Although it's probably best that I didn't know, or I'd have lost sight of my clients' needs and focused on tormenting you instead. However." He spread his fingers in a jazz-hands gesture. "Never too late, as they say."

Taj glared up at him. "What's that supposed to mean?"

"That means if you don't want to end up back in Sheol by defaulting on your business loan, you'll do what I say. Because if you *do* default, I guarantee that I'll win the auction for your services, and now that I know your dirty little secret and I'm prevented from seeking any new clients? I'll be at leisure to torment you 24/7. Forever."

"Trust me," Taj muttered, "that's not the worst that could happen to me." Then he winced internally. Because he'd just given Naberius the opening he needed. Maybe he hadn't noticed Taj's slip. Taj swiveled his chair to face his computer and pulled up a random spreadsheet. It hardly mattered which one. They were all depressing.

"You'll place this topper on that cake," Naberius murmured into Taj's ear, the hot, sulfurous breath nearly choking him. "Your little bit on the side has my curse in his bones. That means I can make it worse any time I want without incurring any fallout from the tribunal. Pre-existing conditions are exempted."

Taj's fingers froze on the keyboard. "You wouldn't."

"Wouldn't I? It's a matter of pride now. My only failure." He chuckled. "Need more incentive? How about this? Once the curse hits the true target, the false target is released. Curse the wedding cake and your bit on the side is free."

Taj's fingers clenched the sides of his keyboard until he heard the plastic crack. Kiran would be released from his curse? Would Kiran want that? Even from their brief acquaintance, Taj knew—heart and soul deep—that Kiran would never sacrifice someone else, especially his beloved sister, for his own comfort.

"Come on, Tendaji-al-Sefu," Naberius purred. "I named you so appropriately. My sword who got things done. You were my perfect weapon."

"I was a dancer. A singer."

"Choose the weapon to fit the target. I honed you to the finest edge and now look at you." Naberius scoffed. "Dulled by something as mundane as love." He spun Taj's chair, forcing him to face him again. "You'll be doing her a favor, you know. Annemiek."

"Seriously? How in all the hells can you justify that?"

Naberius flicked his claws dismissively. "Her career can't last forever. Humans will start to notice that she's not aging. That'll threaten the Secrecy Pact, and Sheol's got *nothing* on the punishment for Secrecy Pact violations. You're giving her a gift by letting her exit before the worst happens. What better time than now, when she's got a new spouse to keep her busy?"

"She's only twenty-seven. She's got years ahead of her."

Naberius's gaze flicked to the side. "Assuming she doesn't meet with some...accident."

"Naberius," Taj growled.

"Oh, for Lucifer's sake, give it up. I've got your balls in a vise and you know it." He tapped his beak with one claw. "Now that I think of it, that might be something I'll do *literally* once you're my minion again."

"I'd rather jump in the lava river than be your minion again."

"As if that would hurt you. You're a *demon*, Tendaji. You're impervious to heat or to anything other than what's inflicted by me." He smirked, and as ever, Taj was mystified how a beak *could* smirk. "Not even the Realm Accords could negate that little issue, not without completely undoing manifestation matrices, which would… Oops!" He put a scaled hand in front of his beak. "End every demon in existence. Not even the self-righteous supe council could countenance genocide."

"I'm not doing it," Taj said between gritted teeth.

"Let me put this another way." Naberius dropped his playful facade. "It's happening. If you do it, your studio becomes a success, you save yourself from eternal torment and your bit on the side from a worsening curse, and Annemiek Bakker's career ends on a high note, just like all my other clients. If *I* do it, however, Annemiek's career will still end, but your studio will close, your bit—"

"He's not my bit on the side. Stop saying that."

"Your *bit* suffers, and so do you. Eternally. Which option sounds like the better deal to you?"

"How about none of the above?"

Naberius ignored him and looked at the clock. "Your bit is late. Once he gets here, encourage him to invite you to the wedding as his plus one."

A little burst of satisfaction broke through Taj's despair. "He's not coming."

The satisfaction grew at the surprise on Naberius's face. "What?" he squawked.

"He canceled. Sorry." *Not sorry.* Well, he was in that he wouldn't see Kiran again, maybe not ever, but definitely not sorry that Kiran was out of Naberius's reach.

"Hmmm." He huffed. "You'll just have to go in as waitstaff then."

"I'm not going in at all!" Taj roared.

"Oh, you're going in," Naberius gloated. "Because the needs of the many outweigh the needs of the one."

"You're misquoting. Besides, you're all about the needs of the one—*your* needs."

"Well, of course," Naberius said, no irony in his tone whatsoever. "Who else's matter?"

Chapter Eight

The weather on Annemiek's wedding day was going to be perfect. Even though it was barely past dawn, the sun just peeking over the hills east of Wildwood Lake, Kiran could tell.

He floated peacefully on the water, its surface only ruffled by a slight breeze as he watched Annemiek wheel and dip in the air overhead, her white feathers tinged pink in the sunrise.

She dove, back-winging to land gracefully beside him, and though they couldn't communicate with words while they were shifted, her happiness and contentment radiated from her in a way that warmed Kiran's heart.

She stroked his neck feathers with the top of her head. He returned the favor, but then turned to paddle toward the secluded inlet, hidden from the view of other resort guests, where the owners had installed a rustic changing room.

Not all Wildwood celebrations were for supes, or supe-only, Annemiek and Del's wedding being a case in point, so the owners had made accommodations to allow privacy when their supe guests needed to indulge their extra-normal natures.

Kiran waddled onto the shore, the relative grace he still maintained while swimming disappearing once he was clear of the water. After he shifted back to his human form, dried off, and donned his sweatpants and T-shirt, he rejoined Annemiek on the path to the resort.

She was wearing oversized sweatpants, the cuffs rolled up to her shins, and a Hunter's Moon hoodie, which Kiran took to be Del's, gazing out over the water with a dreamy expression. When Kiran stumbled to a stop next to her, she linked her arm with his.

"Thanks for coming out here with me this morning. I really needed it."

"Pre-wedding jitters?"

She lifted both eyebrows. "What do you think?"

"I think...that seems unlike you. You've been looking forward to this, to marrying Del, to being with them, almost since you two met."

"Correct." She sighed. "I just needed to get away from the rest of the fuss for a while. It was bad enough last night at the rehearsal dinner, with Dad and Carolee acting as though they were some kind of dueling nightmare wedding planners and attempting to micromanage every minute. I mean, the New Repertory company, both performers and staff, is mostly human, so I'm always careful, on guard against giving away my nature. You'd think that the stress of rehearsing, performing, *touring* in mixed company would have prepared me for this kind of circus."

Kiran smiled at her aggravated tone as they strolled along the edge of the lake. "I've always thought that the *idea* of a fancy wedding is far rosier than the tortured reality of pulling one off. If you'd wanted a smaller ceremony with only family and supe friends, we could have—"

"Bite your tongue," she said, eyes wide in mock outrage. "My best friend is human. Do you honestly think I could get married without having Sandrine as an attendant? Carolee would never forgive me."

Kiran chuckled as they emerged from the woods onto the wide swath of lawn next to the resort lodge. "It's your wedding. Yours and Del's. Not hers. And not Dad's."

"I know." She wrinkled her nose. "Can you believe that Dad is *still* trying to get me to let him partner me in the pre-dinner dance instead of you? He pecked at me all evening." She gazed out at the lake. "Another reason I needed some swan therapy with you this morning."

"Any time, sweetie." He kissed the top of her head. "Any time at all."

When they reached the steps leading to the wide deck overlooking the lake, she kissed his cheek. "I'd better go face the music—and Carolee. I probably won't see you before the ceremony." She rolled her eyes. "The nearlyweds have to remain sequestered from one another until then."

Kiran shrugged. "Tradition?"

"Can't escape that with Carolee around." She grinned. "Why do you think I insisted on a morning wedding? Less time to be away from Del." She leaned closer. "Don't tell Carolee," she whispered, "but Sandrine covered for me when I snuck out to be with them last night. The lake is *very* romantic in the moonlight."

He chuckled. "Your secret is safe with me."

She smiled brightly and ran up the stairs to disappear through Wildwood's heavy oak doors.

Kiran followed more slowly, holding onto the rails, because the last thing he wanted to do was take a tumble mere hours before the ceremony. The lobby was already bustling with activity even though the ceremony wouldn't happen until ten: resort staff setting up the ballroom for the post wedding brunch, guests who'd chosen to stay the night wandering down for breakfast at the buffet set out on the deck, Hunter's Moon roadies packing instruments and amps in from the band's van before it had to be moved to the gravel lot behind a screen of Doug firs.

Kiran spotted his father walking down the stairs and immediately detoured to the elevator. If Bernhard had been pestering Annemiek at the rehearsal dinner, he'd have no qualms cornering Kiran this morning, and Kiran still had things to do.

After his shower, clad in only his boxer briefs, Kiran opened the closet and studied his magical shoes. He sighed. They were red again. Really, really red, despite the black shoe dye he'd hit them with the morning after he'd gotten them from Ronnie Purl, and despite the multiple times he'd slathered them with black shoe polish since.

Right after each treatment, they still didn't look all that great—a little smeary, and when he buffed them, some of the red peeked through around the seams in the uppers. But a couple of hours later, they'd be red again. Consequently, he had to time this exactly right.

He glanced out his window at the willow bower twined with ivy and jasmine that stood below the lodge, overlooking the lake, where the ceremony would take place. As one of Annemiek's attendants, along with Sandrine, Kiran would need to be downstairs, ready to go, by nine-thirty. Carolee had decreed that as a man, he would *not* be allowed to help Annemiek get dressed, thank you very much—another reason they'd gone for their shifted swim this morning—so he was free until then.

Pulling a chair over to the window, he settled down with his laptop, making sure everything was in place for the honeymoon trip, and ignoring his father's multiple phone calls. Luckily, since Bernhard preferred to spend as little time with Kiran as possible, he didn't pound on the door and demand admittance.

At nine, Kiran polished the shoes again. They were black...ish. Smeary blackish, but better that than red. Even if the shoes performed as advertised—and Kiran suspected Ronnie had oversold their effect more than a little—he wanted to draw as little attention as possible to his feet.

He donned his tux, and, with the shoes in a soft terrycloth bag, he peeked out his door. With the suites for the rest of the wedding party in the opposite wing, the coast was clear, so Kiran crept along the balcony overlooking the lobby and took the elevator down.

Since he wouldn't have time to go up to his room to change his shoes after the ceremony—he only had Annemiek and Del's dance to prepare—he slipped into the cloakroom near the entrance to the ballroom and tucked the bag in the corner behind a cardboard box labeled, appropriately enough, *Shoe trees*.

Then he crept back across the room, bumping into a coatrack in a rattle of hangers. "Sorry," he muttered, then gave himself a mental facepalm. "Great. Now I'm apologizing to furniture."

He eased the door closed behind him, heaved a relieved breath, turned around, and ran smack into...

"Taj?"

Taj clutched a pile of tablecloths to his chest. "K-Kiran?"

An adorable wrinkle appeared between Kiran's eyebrows, which, like his beard, were a couple of shades darker than his hair. "What are you doing—oh." A smile dispelled the wrinkle, and Taj had to grip the cloths tighter to resist kissing that delectable curve. "You wear glasses."

Taj touched the earpiece involuntarily. "Um, yes. My, uh, contacts were giving me trouble." Actually, no witch, magician, or druid had been able to embed the vision spells into contacts without melting them, so any demon who expected to function in the Upper World had to wear bespelled spectacles—unless they had special lighting installed, of course.

"You didn't tell me you'd be at the wedding. Do you know Del?"

Taj shook his head. "I'm..." He brandished the tablecloths, which would need a touchup after he'd wrinkled them in his chokehold. "...with the caterers."

Kiran frowned. "The caterers? But you're a dancer. A teacher. Why would you—" He bit his lip, his gaze dropping to the floor. "I'm sorry. It's none of my business."

"It's okay." Every synapse firing along Taj's nerves urged him to take Kiran into his arms, an urge he had to resist. *Thank all the hells for tablecloths.* They made for flimsy armor, but they were better than nothing. "Like I told you, you were my one and only student, so I have to pick up extra work where I can find it." *Liar, liar, liar.* He wasn't getting a dime for this gig. Even if it had been offered—if the caterers realized he was here, which his misdirection ability should prevent—he wouldn't have taken it. It was too much like blood money.

"I'm sorry I had to cancel our last lesson." Kiran lifted his hands in an apologetic shrug, but he still didn't meet Taj's eyes. "A last-minute wedding emergency. You know how it is."

"Sure. Don't worry about it." Taj licked his lips. This is where he could offer to deliver that lesson later, maybe after a nice dinner as a prelude to full naked body contact. But after today, that wouldn't be an option.

One way or another.

"Kiran!" An older man with Kiran's nose and build, but without Kiran's appealing sweetness, beckoned peremptorily from the staircase. "The party is lining up. The least you can do is be on time." He stalked off without bothering to see if Kiran would follow.

Instead of being cowed, though, Kiran just rolled his eyes and chuckled. "My father. I'd introduce you, but I like you too much to inflict that on you." He smiled again, rather tentatively. "I have to go. But maybe I'll see you later?"

Taj held up the tablecloths again. "I don't think I'll be allowed to mingle with the guests, but thank you. Wish your sister and her spouse-to-be the best from me, all right?"

Kiran nodded. "Of course."

Despite desperately wanting to watch Kiran for every possible minute, Taj turned away. He strode toward the ballroom as confidently as if he belonged there, but before he reached the door, two men stepped into his path.

"Could we have a word, please?" the taller of the two said. His dark hair was swept back in a deceptively simple style that Taj recognized as being the result of a very expensive haircut, and his dark suit fit his broad-shouldered form as if he'd been tailored into it directly.

"This way." The shorter man was wearing a tux that matched Kiran's, his thin face earnest and his dark curls rioting around his head.

They both wore glasses that glinted with demon vision spells.

Busted.

Taj followed the two into a neat office. The taller man closed the door. "I'm Quentin Bertrand-Harrington, Wildwood's owner."

"Ah." Taj knew the name. "Incubus."

Quentin inclined his head. "Exactly."

"Taj Sekani. How did you spot me?"

The smaller man said, "That was me. Zeke Oz." He spread his palms. "I was a minion too, so I can recognize another when I see one." He glanced over his shoulder at the closed door. "I don't have much time. The ceremony is about to start and if I'm not there, Hamish will drive Del to distraction." He smiled, nearly as sweetly as Kiran. "My boyfriend and I are Del's attendants."

Quentin smiled fondly at the other man. "Don't worry, Zeke. This won't take long." He fixed Taj with an intense stare. "There won't be any trouble today. Will there?"

Taj swallowed. "I..." He couldn't lie. He couldn't even redirect, not with two other demons.

Zeke put a hand on his arm. "I can see that your desires are tangled. But please know that you have options. If you need any help with your Upper World transition, you can come to me or Quentin." He nodded at the incubus. "He's an advocate, and he's got tons of experience negotiating with the Sheol C-suite and middle management."

Taj's throat thickened. He couldn't have spoken if he'd wanted to, not with these men being so kind. Not with that damnable cursed cake topper practically burning a hole in his dimensional storage pocket. So he nodded.

Zeke beamed at him. "Good. Now I've got to run."

"As do I." Quentin smiled crookedly. "My husband and I are the de facto wedding planners, and since he's so good-natured he'll let anybody do anything, it's up to me to play bad cop." His expression darkened. "Remember, please, Taj. This is a mixed event. I'll take any Secrecy Pact infraction on my premises very poorly. Very poorly indeed."

The two of them disappeared out the door, leaving Taj with his stack of tablecloths and a swirling cloud—hells, a veritable *tornado*—of guilt. *Guess I have a decision to make.*

He left the office. The *real* catering staff was setting up the hors d'oeuvres on the deck. As Taj understood it, immediately after the ceremony, Annemiek and Del would have their first dance in the ballroom, followed by the special dance with a significant person in their lives— Kiran, in Annemiek's case. Afterward, the newlyweds and their guests would proceed to the deck for mimosas and appetizers before returning to the ballroom for cake cutting, brunch, and dancing.

When he marched into the ballroom with his crumpled tablecloths, it was empty of any other person. Through the bank of French doors on one side of the room, he could see the wedding procession heading toward the lakeside bower and the waiting officiant. He winced a little when Kiran stumbled, but was steadied by Zeke.

My fault.

He took a deep breath and walked toward the long table where the five-tiered wedding cake stood in pride of place among a scatter of iris and yellow chrysanthemums.

It wasn't fair, damn it to all the hells. Why must an innocent party suffer—Kiran, Annemiek, Taj himself—because of Naberius's ego and some random person's selfishness? Taj snorted. He could hardly count himself as innocent, could he? Not after so many centuries as Naberius's dogsbody.

With one final glance out the window, he reached into the dimensional pocket and closed his hand around the cake topper.

Chapter Nine

The ceremony was perfect, the sun on the lake no brighter than the expressions on Del and Annemiek's faces as they promised to love and care for each other forever.

Kiran sniffed a little as the officiant pronounced them married. Sandrine nudged him with her elbow and, with a grin, passed him a tissue from the packet she had hidden behind her bouquet.

"Thanks," he murmured.

"Don't mention it," she replied, dabbing her own eyes. Then an exasperated expression flickered over her face and she glanced over her shoulder at where Carolee was tweaking the hem of her yellow satin dress. "Mama," she whispered, "what are you doing?"

"Your skirt isn't hanging straight," Carolee said under cover of the other guests' cheers and applause. "It looks just awful."

"Nobody's looking at *me*," Sandrine said, turning her mother gently around and pushing her toward the crowd surrounding Annemiek and Del. "It's not my wedding. Now go congratulate the newlyweds." She shook her head as Carolee marched away, the lavender fascinator in her silvering blond hair bouncing with her determined steps. Sandrine winked at Kiran. "I don't think my mother has ever recovered from her days as the most forceful dance mom in the Pacific Northwest."

Kiran chuckled. "You have to admit, she was really good at it."

"Yes, but I haven't danced in years." She lifted the hem of her gown to display a pair of bedazzled Doc Martens. "I much prefer being able to walk, thank you very much." She winked again and patted her curvy hips. "And to eat what I want. No matter what my mother says, I'm having a really big slice of Del and Anni's wedding cake. Maybe two. *And* sufficient champagne to make me tipsy enough to make a fool of myself with one of the cute servers."

Kiran wouldn't mind finding one cute server in particular and dragging him into the nearest closet. Although he wouldn't want to jeopardize Taj's job. *He shouldn't be moonlighting with random caterers. He should be dancing.* Or teaching other dancers.

Speaking of dancing…

The butterflies in Kiran's belly that had calmed during the ceremony swarmed up his ribcage. "Sandrine, if Anni looks for me, could you please tell her I've gone to change my shoes for our d-dance?" He gulped. "I'll meet her in the ballroom."

"Sure thing, Kir." She gave him a one-armed hug. "Don't worry. You'll do great." Her smile was kind. "She just wants to share this moment with you. If you do nothing but stand in place and sway a little, it'll be enough."

He nodded, his throat thick, and skulked away from the crowd surrounding the newlyweds, earning a disapproving glance from his father. *So what else is new?*

Kiran detoured through the lobby because Hunter's Moon was already tuning up in the ballroom, and the caterers were busy on the deck, pouring mimosas and plating appetizers. He made it to the cloakroom with no more than the standard number of stumbles, trips, and wall collisions.

The shoes were right where he'd left them, still blackish...mostly. When he slid his left foot into the first one, the contrast with his trouser leg was noticeable. *Very* noticeable. *Who knew black came in so many different colors?*

Oh, well. It would all be over soon.

He slipped on the other shoe and tied the laces in double knots, just to be sure. When he stood, the difference was immediately apparent: He felt so light that he was surprised he didn't float up to the ceiling. He tried a simple box step and his smile bloomed into a full-on grin.

"Look at me," he said, trying a pas de bourrée and succeeding, "I'm dancing."

A laugh burbled in his chest and he practically skipped —no, not practically, he *actually* skipped out of the cloakroom, across the lobby, and into the ballroom, where Del and Annemiek were just taking the floor to Hunter's Moon's signature tune, *Lover's Reel.*

Their steps were fast and intricate—Del was just as quick on their feet as Annemiek—and the two of them switched leads every few measures, exemplifying the give and take in their relationship that made them such a perfect match.

Standing at the edge of the dance floor with the other guests, Kiran swayed and shuffled along with the beat— which didn't really stand out since everyone else was swaying and shuffling, too. They couldn't help it, given that Hunter's Moon's lead singer was the last true bard in Faerie: When Gareth Kendrick sang, *everybody* danced. The unusual thing about Kiran joining in was that he didn't bump into anybody else. Not even once.

Magical shoes are the best!

Annemiek spun Del into a final dip, and they laughed gently before executing a complicated reversal so that Del dipped Annemiek instead. Kiran sighed happily. *True partners.* Exactly what he'd always wished for his little sister.

What he'd wished for himself too, if he were honest, but Kiran was nothing if not a realist. In order to find your true partner, you had to actually look, and that wasn't really on his schedule.

But there's Taj.

For Taj, maybe Kiran could *make* time in his schedule.

On the dance floor, Zeke, the adorable demon whose kangaroo shifter boyfriend was Hunter's Moon's drummer and who'd been one of Del's attendants, stepped forward to take Del's hand. *Showtime.*

Kiran stepped—no, *chasséed*—forward to take Annemiek in his arms as the band struck up another, slower tune, probably to take pity on the non-dancers in this event. But as he led Annemiek in that same triple turn that had so stolen Kiran's breath when Taj had partnered him in the studio, he wanted to shout, *Ha! There are no non-dancers here!*

Annemiek gazed up at him, a bemused expression on her face. "Kir? What is happening right now?"

"We're dancing." He grinned and let the shoes do their thing, a grapevine step while he passed Annemiek from one arm to the other.

"I see that," she said with a giggle as he spun her out and back. "But how?"

"I took lessons." He held her close and rested his cheek against her hair as they cha-cha-ed around Del and Zeke. "I wanted this day to be perfect for you. I didn't want to embarrass you or Del."

"Oh, Kir," she said, an obvious catch in her voice as she leaned back to look up at him. "It would have been perfect if all we did was stand here unmoving. I just wanted to have this moment with you, the most important person in my life other than Del." She kissed his cheek—a neat trick since the shoes had decided to switch to a waltz, but then, Annemiek was a professional. "To let you know that won't change."

"I love you too, Anni," he murmured. "I think—"

Rrrriiip.

"I'm sorry. I'm so sorry," Zeke babbled. "I wasn't watching where I was going." Zeke's pale face was blotched with red. "Your beautiful dress, Anni."

Annemiek glanced behind her at her skirt, even though Kiran didn't stop their swing step sequence. "Oh."

"Not to worry, Zeke," Del said. "The flounce just came loose. Easily fixed."

Sandrine hurried over to help, but Carolee brushed past her. "I've got my sewing kit up in the dressing room. Come along and we'll have it fixed in a jiffy."

She practically had to yank Annemiek out of Kiran's arms because he hadn't stopped dancing with her, not even though the band had cut off the song in the middle,

Hamish leaping out from behind his drum kit to comfort Zeke.

Kiran tried to stop dancing. He really did, even going so far as to aim for the nearest obstacle—a satin upholstered chair—to instigate a collision on purpose. But he neatly sidestepped it and then leaped over its neighbor's seat in a grand jeté that made his eyes pop wide when he landed it perfectly.

Sweat prickled along his hairline. People were starting to notice. His father was glaring at him. Quentin, the resort owner, was gazing at him with concern, his brow pleated above his glasses. Some of the guests—especially the human ones—were staring and tittering. Only Del was regarding him with apparent satisfaction, a faint smile on their lips.

If I can't stop dancing, maybe I can at least redirect.

He set his jaw and, with memories of his single disastrous tap lesson playing in his mind, determinedly shuffled off to Buffalo—and out the ballroom doors.

The stack of plates in Taj's hands clattered and his jaw sagged as he stared at the man—at *Kiran*—dancing across the lobby like a fusion of Fred Astaire and Nappytabs.

What the...

Had Kiran been feigning clumsiness? But why? There was no reason for that. Taj winced and mentally kicked himself in the ass. *Stupid.* That was impossible, not only because Kiran wasn't the kind of man to indulge in subterfuge, but because now that Taj knew what to look for, he could detect the shadow of Naberius's touch on Kiran's *calon*. The signature shadow was unmistakable, and Taj should know. He'd helped deliver enough of them, although Naberius's standard victim was human, not supe.

As Kiran executed a complicated lock step, followed by a double pirouette, Taj focused on Kiran's shoes. They weren't the ones Taj had sold him. This pair was different. Malevolent. Cursed.

And also really, really red.

"Damn it to all the hells," Taj muttered, and ditched the plates behind a potted ficus. As he hurried across the lobby, Kiran was fumbling with the cloakroom door handle while also leaping in the air to click his heels together.

Taj caught him mid-leap and shoved the door open, carrying Kiran inside with his feet doing changements in the air, kicking Taj's shins with every shift of his legs.

"I'm sorry," Kiran whimpered. "Did I hurt you?"

"Never mind that," Taj said through gritted teeth as he set Kiran on the floor, hands gripping his shoulders in an attempt—a failed attempt—to hold him in place. "What in the hells are you doing with cursed shoes?"

Kiran's eyes widened before his gaze shifted away from Taj's. "Cursed? There's no such thing as—"

"Give it up, Kiran. I know a curse when I see one." He caught Kiran's chin and turned his head so their eyes met. "I'm a demon."

Kiran blinked. "You... What?"

"I said, I'm a demon. And you're a swan shifter. A swan shifter who's wearing gods-bedamned *cursed shoes*. So I ask you again, what are you doing with them?"

Kiran was hopping under Taj's hands like Michael Flatley in *Lord of the Dance*. "I didn't know... I just wanted to dance with Anni. To not ruin her day." He scowled up at Taj as he did a pas de chat. "You have no room to talk. *You've* got magical shoes, too. You told me so."

Taj was torn between horror and the urge to laugh. "They're magical because they're *comfortable.* They have to be if I'm to be dancing in them all day. They're not actually bespelled. And they're certainly not cursed." He glanced down at Kiran's feet, now in sous-sus. "Nor are they red."

"I *tried* to cover that up, but the polish kept wearing off."

"Of course it wore off. The shoes are *cursed.*"

"Stop saying that," Kiran grumbled. "I get it, okay?"

"So take them off, Kiran." Taj stared into his eyes. "Take off the damned red shoes."

"I can't," Kiran wailed. "I can't stop dancing long enough to unlace them. Every time I try to reach them, they send me into some really complicated sequence."

"Guess we'll have to get creative then." He let go of Kiran's shoulders, only to have him do a tour en l'air. "Can you do an arabesque?"

"*I* can't do one." He glared down at his feet. "But I'm pretty sure the shoes can."

Sure enough, Kiran swiveled, his left leg extending behind him, and Taj seized the opportunity, pressing Kiran above his head and pacing across the cloakroom. Luckily, the ceilings were high, so Kiran didn't bash his head on the exposed beams.

"Kiran," he murmured, uncertain whether the shoes could respond to verbal cues as well as physical ones, "don't be alarmed, but when I lower you, I'm going to pivot and press your back against the wall."

"Okay," Kiran said shakily.

"Then I want you to wrap your legs around my waist. Can you do that?"

Kiran peered down at him. "Is that a trick question?"

Taj chuckled. "Perfectly legit, I promise."

"All right."

"Ready?" At Kiran's nod, Taj let him drop into a fish hold, Kiran's head down and his passé perfect. Then, with muscles honed over years of partnering dancers of all shapes and sizes, Taj flipped Kiran up and pressed him against the wall. Kiran, trouper that he was, wrapped his legs around Taj's hips.

Then, despite the time steps pummeling his ass, Taj reached back and ripped off first one shoe and then the other.

"Ow!" Kiran said.

"Sorry."

"Don't be." Kiran took a deep breath. "Gods, that feels wonderful."

"Yeah, being forced to dance when you don't want to is the worst." Taj knew from experience.

Kiran smiled at him, slow and sly. "I wasn't talking about the absence of cursed footwear." He cupped Taj's cheek with one hand. "I'm talking about you. *You* feel wonderful."

"So do you," Taj croaked.

Kiran slid his hands behind Taj's head and laced his fingers together, cool and soothing against Taj's skin. Then Kiran's lips were on his. Soft. Enticing. *Arousing.*

Taj moaned and pressed harder against Kiran as Kiran linked his ankles together at the small of Taj's back.

When Kiran parted his lips, Taj teased inside that delectable mouth with the tip of his tongue. Their natures were opposite—fire and water—but clearly that wasn't a drawback, because Kiran was respite and solace and refuge.

And the other thing about fire and water? When they met...

Steam.

"Tell me," Kiran panted between kisses along Taj's throat, "would it be tacky to suck you off at my sister's wedding?"

Taj's cock throbbed, and he laughed breathlessly. "I'm pretty sure tacky, inappropriate hookups at weddings are SOP."

Kiran drew back, peering into Taj's eyes worriedly. "Do you think this is inappropriate? I mean, I admit it might be impulsive." He gave Taj a heated look as he trailed a finger along his jaw. "Although I doubt anyone who sees you would blame me. But do you? Think it's inappropriate?"

"Kiran—"

"I mean, you're a supe. I'm a supe. There's no reason why we, um, can't date." Uncertainty flickered across his face. "Right?"

Taj's breath caught. "Do *you* want to date *me*?"

Kiran's smile wobbled. "Well, of course. I don't make out in closets with just *anyone*, but you and I seem to be making a habit of it. One might almost say a tradition." He must have caught the regret in Taj's expression. "Unless *you* don't want to date *me*. Do you? Taj?"

The uncertainty in Kiran's tone nearly ripped out Taj's heart. "That's not it." He swallowed. "I've got something to tell you, and after you hear it, I'm pretty sure you'll never want to see me again."

Chapter Ten

Kiran peered into Taj's face, studying the desolation in his dark eyes, the pinch of pain around his full lips. "I promise there's not much you could say that would make me—"

"Wait. Don't make any promises until you hear the truth." He smiled crookedly. "You should know better than to make promises to a demon, anyway. That never ends well."

Kiran snorted. "That depends on the demon. And also what it is I'm promising. My back may be against the wall here"—he wriggled to emphasize the way they were connected, hip to hip, their cocks nestled against one another behind the relatively flimsy shield of cotton underwear and black wool—"but my soul is not on the table." *Although I'm pretty sure my heart is a done deal.* "Besides, since the Realm Accords, aren't demons and angels all just members of the Host on a sliding scale of self-aggrandizement?"

"Semantics." Taj glanced down at their groins. "Maybe we should…separate for this conversation." Although the way his arms tightened around Kiran's waist, he probably didn't want distance between them any more than Kiran did.

"I don't think so." He brushed his hand over the skin of Taj's head, fascinated as ever by its smoothness. "I like it right here."

Taj clenched his eyes shut. "Kiran—"

"*Taj*," Kiran said, matching Taj's exasperated tone and raising it by an order of magnitude. "Just tell me, okay?"

For a moment, Kiran thought Taj would refuse. But then he nodded, his Adam's apple sliding under the smooth skin of his throat. Since it was *right there*, Kiran pressed a kiss to it.

"Tell me. I promise to listen."

"That's all I could ask for." Taj dropped his forehead against Kiran's shoulder, as though he couldn't look into Kiran's eyes as he spoke. "About twenty years ago, at my progenitor's orders, I delivered a ballerina birthday cake loaded with more sparkles and piped pink frosting than should be allowed to a house in the Portland West Hills."

Kiran stopped stroking Taj's head. "On Elizabeth Street?"

Taj nodded, his cheek brushing Kiran's beard. "A cursed cake. A cursed cake aimed at a *child*." He lifted his head, and *gods*, the pain in his eyes. "I didn't know, but I *should* have. Naberius—my progenitor—had never done anything like it before. He focused solely on adults in the performing arts because he was eaten up with envy for their careers. But I should have *known*. What adult wants a pink ballerina cake covered in purple sparkles?"

Kiran cupped Taj's jaw. "If this is going where I think it's going, I'll tell you at least one *child* who didn't want that cake." He fixed Taj with a glare. "Annemiek Nicoline Bakker, that's who. She wanted a pirate cake."

"Kiran, you don't get it. I didn't stay to make sure the curse landed as intended. I just delivered the cake and high-tailed it back to my other assignment, which was rehearsing Riff in a touring production of *West Side Story*, and making the understudy so jealous he'd be ready to sell his soul to Naberius to have me break an ankle on opening night."

Kiran lifted his eyebrows. "Did that kind of thing happen often?"

"All the time, but you're not *listening*. That curse landed on *you*. I didn't notice at first when you arrived at the studio because I was so blinded by...well...you."

Despite himself, Kiran felt his belly—and points south —warm at Taj's confession. "You were attracted to me at first sight?"

"Of *course* I was." Taj's hands tightened on Kiran's hips, and Kiran had a feeling if Taj had hair, he'd be pulling it out now. "But when Naberius confessed, I could *see* it. See the cloud on your *calon*." He gave a disgusted snort. "I couldn't see it before because the lights in the studio mask all my demon abilities. I insisted on it."

"Light Fantastic," Kiran murmured. "It's not just a play on an obscure John Milton quote. It's a declaration of freedom. A celebration of your emergence into the Upper World."

"Yes, but that's not the point. I didn't stay that day, and *you* ate the first bite of that cursed cake."

Kiran huffed a laugh. "I didn't just eat the first bite, Taj. I ate the whole blasted thing and was sick as a dog afterward."

It was Taj's turn to raise his eyebrows. "The *whole cake*? Why?"

Kiran smiled wryly. "Because I heard them. The person who wanted the curse—Tanglefoot, they called it—and the person who cast it."

"Naberius," Taj said glumly.

"I couldn't hear them clearly, or I could have saved myself a bellyache, but I heard enough." He cradled Taj's face between his hands. "I didn't eat that cake by accident, or through jealousy or greed, the way my father has always believed. I ate it intentionally, so the curse would fall on me and not my sister."

Taj blinked, and Kiran couldn't tell if his expression was awe or total WTF. "You knew about the curse? And invoked it anyway?"

Kiran nodded. "I'd do it again, too. Yes, I'm clumsy and awkward and should have bought stock in every bandage company in the country, but I have no regrets. Maybe I can't fly—"

"You can't fly?" Taj's voice cracked on the last word.

"But I can still shift. I can still swim next to my sister and watch *her* fly. I can watch her *dance*. And that's worth it."

"But, Kiran—"

"Taj, did you have a choice? If you had known, could you have refused?"

"I could have chosen eternal torment," Taj muttered.

Kiran smiled and stroked Taj's cheek. "I think you did. Guilt is one of the worst torments I can think of."

"But you can't *fly*."

"No. But Anni can dance. And that's a tradeoff I can live with." He snorted. "Although to my father, to Carolee, I'll always be the boy who was so jealous of his sister that he ate her birthday cake. But I haven't been that boy for twenty years."

"You were never that boy."

Kiran shook his head. "Taj, our past actions shouldn't limit our lives, not if we're committed to doing the right thing now and in the future. My father's opinions are based on false assumptions that I don't choose to correct. The things you were forced to do as a minion shouldn't define you now that you're free." He kissed Taj softly. "Live in your fantastic light, Taj. It's time."

"I don't know how you can say that," Taj said miserably. "How you can forgive me."

Kiran shrugged. "There's nothing to forgive. Being cursed hasn't precisely been a picnic, but it's not the worst thing in the world and I've adapted. If you walk away? Simply because you think you don't deserve happiness? Now *that* would be bad."

"You..." Taj shook his head. "You're incredible."

Heat infused Kiran's cheeks. "No. Just pragmatic. I've gotten very good at creative problem solving as I found ways to work around the curse."

Taj winced. "That's probably good, because it's about to get worse."

Kiran blinked. "What?"

Taj released him, but supported him as he slid down the wall and onto his feet. "Naberius has been manipulating things to make the studio fail. Masking it from sight. That's why you were my first and only student."

Kiran frowned. "Then how did I find that coupon?"

"Because he made sure you got it. *I'd* never seen it before."

"Taj!" Kiran thumped his chest lightly with his closed fist. "You should have said something. Why in the world would you honor it?"

He smiled crookedly and ran a finger down Kiran's cheek. "First and only student, remember? Also I couldn't stand to watch you walk away."

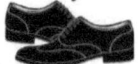

Kiran's gray eyes darkened. "When you say things like that, I want to jump your bones right here and now."

Taj laughed, gripping Kiran's shoulders. "Not that I would mind, but didn't you hear me? Your curse is about to get worse. Naberius didn't send that coupon to some random person. He sent it to *you*."

Kiran blinked. "Me? Why?"

"A combination of ego and contract vagueness. The original client is demanding that the curse be directed properly and land on its intended target at last."

"Annemiek," Kiran breathed, eyes wide in horror.

Taj nodded. "He ordered me to place a cursed cake topper on the wedding cake. Tying up loose ends, he called it. Since this is the last *client* he'll ever be allowed, I suspect he's indulging in a last burst of spiteful muscle flexing because he won't get another shot."

Kiran clutched Taj's biceps, his expression fierce. "You didn't do it. Please tell me you didn't do it."

He placed his hands over Kiran's. "Of course I didn't. But Naberius gave me a choice. I could curse Annemiek, and my studio would succeed. If I refused, it would fail, and I'd be forced to return to Sheol, once again his minion." He gazed into Kiran's eyes, wanting him to understand, to forgive. "And he'd twist your curse harder, increase its effects." He shook his head. "I'm sorry, Kiran. I couldn't do that to Annemiek. Not today, on her wedding day. Not ever. But that means the burden of Naberius's actions falls on you. Again."

"And on you," Kiran cried. "It wasn't your fault, not the first time and not this time. It's whoever's insisting on completing the curse." He threw his arms around Taj and hugged him tight. "Thank you. Thank you for not cursing my sister."

Taj chuckled weakly. "It means you and I have a pretty grim future, my dear."

"I don't care." He gazed into Taj's face. "There are rules in place now. The Realm Accords have contingencies, protocols for appeals and complaints. Naberius might consider this contract still in effect, but I guarantee you the tribunal won't judge it quite so flexibly. Especially since the original curse did land *somewhere.*" He took Taj's hand. "It may take a while, but we'll figure it out."

"You don't know Naberius," Taj muttered as Kiran, still in stockinged feet, drew him toward the door.

"Maybe not. But I know me." He turned back, his hand on the doorknob. "And I don't give up." They emerged into the lobby. "You know, I think Del might have foreseen this."

Anti-grav wasn't one of Taj's demon abilities—Naberius had wanted him to be grounded when he danced—but he felt as though he were floating with Kiran's hand in his. "Foreseen what?"

"That I'd arrive with a previously unscheduled plus-one. There's a place card next to my seat at the head table." He grinned mischievously. "Want to go see if your name's on it?" His grin faded. "Oh, but you're working with the caterers."

Taj tilted an eyebrow at him. "I was only dressed like a caterer. I was here on a stealth mission, remember?"

"Excellent!" He beamed, swinging their joined hands. "Then let's go see." He gazed down at their linked fingers. "You know, it seems like whenever I'm touching you, I'm not as accident-prone."

Taj raised Kiran's hand to his lips and kissed it. "That's because it's Naberius's curse and I was his minion when he cast it. I've got some control over it, enough to negate it while we're in contact." He grimaced. "Not enough to reverse it, though."

Kiran chuckled. "To be honest," he said as they entered the ballroom, empty of guests since everyone was out on the deck being plied with mimosas and small bites, "I'm not sure I'd know how to function if it suddenly disappeared."

Taj smiled down at him. "Knowing you, I'm pretty sure you'd conquer the challenge in no time."

"Maybe, but…" He clutched Taj's arm with his other hand. "Taj. The cake!"

Taj followed the direction of Kiran's horrified gaze. A caterer was about to place the cursed topper on the cake's fifth tier. "Stop!" he shouted and raced toward the table, dragging Kiran along at his side.

The caterer, whose name tag read *Leslie*, stared at them, her jaw sagging. "But—"

"I'll take that, Leslie." Kiran held out his hand.

Leslie glanced from Kiran to the topper. "But the guests will be in soon. And the cake cutting will happen before they sit down for brunch."

"It's all right." Kiran smiled at her encouragingly. "I'm one of the attendants. We have a, er, *special* topper that we'll be presenting to the newlyweds before the first slice."

"O-okay," Leslie said, handing it over. "If anyone asks —"

"Send them to me. Kiran Bakker."

She nodded and hurried away.

Taj took the damned thing out of Kiran's hand. "I swear I didn't leave this lying around. I stowed it in my dimensional storage pock— Naberius," he growled. "Naberius can access that pocket, probably because I bought it on the Sheol secondary market and he installed a back door somehow."

Kiran, of course, was unflappable. "Then we can't put it back there. We have to put it somewhere no one will look." He bit his lip, brow wrinkled in thought for a moment, and Taj waited. Because he had total faith that Kiran would come up with a solution.

Sure enough, Kiran snapped his fingers, his smile blooming. "Come on." He tugged on Taj's hand and, despite being in stockinged feet on the polished wood floor, didn't slip or trip as he led Taj back to the cloakroom.

When they stepped inside, Kiran's cursed red shoes were lying in the middle of the room, one on its side and the other upside down. He grabbed one and held it out. "Put it in here."

A surprised laugh bubbled out of Taj's throat. "Are you serious?"

"Why not? Curse with curse. Seems appropriate. Unless…" A worry wrinkle appeared between his brows. "They can't, you know, *breed*, can they?"

Taj almost lost it at the mental image of the red shoes, one cake topper figure upright in each, tip-tapping across the ballroom floor. "N-no. No breeding."

"Good. Then do it."

Kiran steadied the shoe while Taj shoved the topper inside. "I'm surprised it fits. It's not exactly the same size or shape as your foot."

Kiran grinned. "Cursed shoes, remember? They're guaranteed to fit." He frowned at the shoe's mate, lying on the floor. "Although I don't trust them anywhere near each other. Let's go."

Once again, Taj let Kiran take the lead. He towed Taj across the lobby and onto the wide front porch. The double doors were flanked by potted sweet bay shrubs. Kiran glanced from the shoe in his hand to the soil under one plant's bushy branches.

"Allow me," Taj said, and flexed his free hand to extend his claws.

Kiran's look of admiration warmed Taj to his toes. "Very convenient. Remind me to ask about your other demon attributes later."

Taj waggled his eyebrows as he scooped a hole at the edge of the pot. "You mean my *Host* attributes?"

Kiran laughed. "That's the spirit." He plunged the shoe into the hole, and Taj smoothed the dirt over it.

"I hope the dual curses don't kill the plant."

"Don't worry," Kiran said, "I know a dryad who can take care of it if necessary. Let's go wash our hands and check out that place setting, because if it *doesn't* have your name, I intend to reword the card myself." He wiggled the fingers of his free hand. "I may have issues with large motor skills, but my manual dexterity *rocks*."

Chapter Eleven

Their time in the restroom wasn't entirely taken up with hand-washing. Kiran hadn't resisted when Taj urged him into one of the stalls. Gods, Taj's mouth, so hot and sweet. His scent, like a campfire on a cold day. His body, so hard and perfect. *My other half.* Kiran could only hope Taj felt the same.

They were both a little breathless and, yes, giggly, when they emerged.

"I hope everybody's still busy out on the deck," Kiran whispered as they crossed the lobby. "I'd hate to have to explain to anyone where I've been."

"Or why your lips look like they've been kissed."

"Well, that's an easy one to answer," he said with a wink. "Because they have." His fingers tightened on Taj's hand. "I'm not hiding you. Not hiding us." Kiran's belly took a nosedive. "I mean…I don't want to if you don't. Is that okay?"

Taj's gentle smile and the kiss he dropped on Kiran's hair were all the answer Kiran needed. But he used his words too. "More than okay. I'm proud to be seen with you."

The tension in Kiran's shoulders released. "Thank all the gods," he said as they entered the ballroom, "because…" For the first time since he'd taken Taj's hand, he stumbled.

Because Carolee was jamming the cursed topper onto the cake, muttering, "If you want something done right, you have to do it yourself."

Kiran yanked Taj behind a giant ficus. "Carolee," Kiran croaked. "*Carolee* was the curser? But why?"

Taj's jaw tightened. "I can guess. Naberius said the curse was on behalf of another person. The client wanted something for someone else."

"Sandrine," Kiran said disgustedly. "She always lost the lead roles, the plum solos, to Anni. Sandrine didn't care. She danced for fun." He gazed up at Taj. "For joy, like you said in that first lesson. It was never her passion." He peered through the leaves. Carolee was regarding the cake, her arms akimbo. She gave a little nod of satisfaction, and that little nod broke something loose inside Kiran.

This woman had been their friend. A maternal figure after their own mother had passed. Annemiek had spent as much time at the McIlhenny house as she had at their own. And all that time, Carolee had resented Annemiek's success? Seethed because she'd avoided the curse? Was scheming to make sure it landed at last?

"Come on." He tugged on Taj's hand, trying to pull him out from behind the ficus.

"Are you sure?"

"She wanted to curse my seven-year-old sister, and now she wants to curse my twenty-seven-year-old sister on her fricking *wedding day*. Of *course* I'm sure."

"Then I'm right behind you."

Kiran marched toward Carolee with Taj a solid presence at his side. "Carolee, you—"

"Bless your heart, Kiran," she said with that honeyed—and clearly fake—smile, "y'all shouldn't be anywhere near this cake. What would your daddy say?"

Taj looked down at him, eyebrows raised. "You have a daddy?"

"Not *that* kind," Kiran said. "She means my father." He eyed Carolee. "And I'm pretty sure *bless your heart* is southern-belle speak for *fuck you*."

"Kiran!" Carolee could fake righteous indignation with the best of them. "Such language. What would your mama think?"

"Don't mention her. Not now. Not ever," Kiran said through clenched teeth. "You have no right. You have no right to be at this *wedding*, and if I have anything to say about it, you'll never be within ten *miles* of my sister ever again."

"Don't be silly, Kiran. Who else can she turn to when her own brother is so selfish as to ruin her birthday and is about to do the same to her wedding." She cast a dismissive glance at Taj. "Shouldn't y'all be helping to plate up brunch?"

"I'm on a break," Taj growled.

Carolee sniffed. "Hmmph. It's so hard to get good help anymore. Now." She took Kiran by the arm and spun him around, making him lose his grip on Taj's hand. "I'm afraid I have to insist. A seventh birthday party was one thing, but this is Anni's wedding. She'll take that first bite of cake if I have to lock y'all in the basement to get it done."

In his stockinged feet, Kiran couldn't get any purchase against the polished wood floor as Carolee resolutely propelled him across the ballroom. He banged his hip on the edge of a table and a toe on a chair—twice—before she pushed him into the lobby. She shoved Taj out after him, although given that Taj was nearly twice her size, Kiran suspected he'd come on his own, to offer support.

She slammed the ballroom doors in their faces. Kiran glared at the heavy oak panels. "Why can't she just admit to the damned curse?" He thought back to their conversation. "Why couldn't I accuse her of it?"

Taj shrugged. "Because she's human. The old supe/human limitations didn't apply to demons on a soul-collecting spree, but you're not the demon she contracted with."

"That...makes no sense."

"What can I tell you? It's like Sheol's version of an NDA, only reinforced with magic."

"How did she even *find* the topper? And why wasn't it covered in potting soil?"

Taj's expression darkened. "Naberius, of course. It probably popped up magically in her handbag, or she had a sudden urge to dig in the ornamental foliage. But that doesn't matter. What matters is that we can't let anyone eat that cursed cake."

Kiran thought of the five tiers of chocolate sponge, raspberry filling, and buttercream, and his stomach tried to turn over. "Despite my father's opinion about my cake jones, even *I* couldn't eat that whole thing."

Taj smiled at him fondly, making Kiran's toes curl against the wood floor. "You don't have to eat it, love. Just destroy it."

Kiran smacked his forehead. "Why didn't I think of that the first time?"

"Well, you were ten. When confronted with cake, eating is the default."

"Okay, then." Kiran grasped the door handle, but it wouldn't budge. "She's locked us out. She's probably on the deck now, on guard, making sure I don't get back in."

Taj flicked a finger at his vest and touched his bow tie. "I'm an ersatz caterer, remember? Take off your tux jacket and you could be one too. I'll bet she didn't think about access through the kitchen." His face twisted in disgust. "After all, that's for the *help*."

Kiran stripped off his tux jacket, but before he could fling it on the floor, Taj took it from his hand. "Let's hang this up, shall we? You may want to don it again once we head this curse off."

"Oh. Good point."

They stowed the jacket on a hanger in the cloakroom, Kiran shivering a little at the single red shoe lying balefully in the middle of the floor. "Stop judging me," he muttered, and shut the door firmly behind them.

With Kiran's hand in his, Taj led them down a hallway and through a swinging door into a bustling kitchen. All the caterers and servers—male and female—wore the same white shirts, black vests, trousers, and bow ties. A couple of them glanced at Taj and Kiran curiously, but most were too busy plating the elegant wedding brunch.

They exited through a second swinging door into the empty ballroom. Kiran spotted Carolee in her lavender chiffon dress outside, standing next to Sandrine, who was laughing with Annemiek and Del. He felt a growl rumbling in his chest.

Taj chuckled and tugged Kiran forward. "If I didn't know you were a swan, I'd swear you were a bear or a tiger with that growl."

"I'm a tiger when it comes to my sister. And that bitch is going *down*."

As they stood in front of the cake, Taj could *feel* the curse. It raised the hair on his arms and prickled his scalp. He couldn't see it, of course—not with the special spells on his glasses that blocked his demon perceptions. *Maybe I should get those adjusted.* Because apparently the Upper World held more pitfalls than he'd imagined.

Then he sighed, because his time in the Upper World was probably numbered in hours, if not minutes.

"Once we destroy this, you know what will happen," he murmured, squeezing Kiran's hand.

"Not really. And neither do you." He laid his head on Taj's shoulder. "But do you have any doubt that this is the right thing to do?"

Taj kissed Kiran's soft hair. "Not a one."

"Then we'll cross whatever bridges await us when we come to them." He turned, pivoting Taj so the two of them faced each other, and wrapped his arms around Taj's waist. "But one thing I know for certain. I'm not giving up and leaving you to languish in Sheol. My father may not have a very high opinion of me, but Taj, I'm the financial manager for some of the wealthiest supes in existence, including the vampire clan chief and the brother of the Faerie King."

Taj smiled down at him. "So what you're saying is that you've got connections?"

He nodded. "The best. But can you face life with a guy who'll be even more clumsy than he is now?"

"As long as you can face life with an ex-minion demon with a failing dance studio."

"That's an ex-minion *Host*, if you please." Kiran snorted. "Besides, after Annemiek Bakker endorses your school, you'll have more students than you can shake a toe shoe at."

"Why would Annemiek endorse me?"

He kissed Taj's lips softly, then punctuated the kiss with a little nip. "Because you taught me to dance, of course. She was very impressed by how well I led her."

Taj lifted a brow. "That wasn't my stellar instruction. If I recall correctly, that was courtesy of a pair of cursed red shoes."

"I know that, and you know that, and the ferret shifter who sold the damn things to me knows that, but as far as anybody else is concerned? It was all you, sweetheart." He kissed Taj again. "That's my story, and I'm sticking to it."

Taj caught movement on the deck. "I think our window of opportunity is closing fast. Ready?"

Kiran nodded, and they each eased their fingers under the enormous silver cake platter and slid it toward the edge of the table.

"Ooof. This thing is heavy," Kiran puffed.

"Five tiers. You do the math."

"Kiran!" a man's voice roared. "What are you doing? I warned Annemiek not to trust you around cake."

"Shit," Kiran muttered. "My father."

"Don't y'all worry, Bernhard," Carolee said, her southern drawl extra-pronounced. "I'll take care of this." She marched toward them, a warlike glint in her eye as the rest of the guests, including Del and Annemiek, clustered in the doorways.

"We're not going to be able to carry it out," Taj muttered.

"Then tip and push," Kiran replied. "Now."

They lifted the back edge of the platter and the cake teetered, fighting gravity, as Carolee screeched for them to stop and Bernhard Bakker berated his son. *That shit is going to stop too*, Taj vowed, as gravity won and the cake crashed to the wood floor, marring its gleaming surface with buttercream, chocolate sponge, and raspberry filling. One of the little kids in the crowd darted forward with an avaricious glint in their eye, so Taj crouched quickly and scooped up a hunk of cake topped with a mangled buttercream rosette. He popped it in his mouth.

"What did you do that for?" Kiran asked as chaos surrounded them.

"At least I'm the one who took the first bite. Even if somebody else tastes it later, they'll be safe."

"Oh, Taj." Kiran's voice was broken.

"Don't worry, my dear." He winked. "It's my progenitor's curse. It can't hurt me."

Kiran's eyes narrowed. "Why didn't you say that before? We could have avoided spreading cake entrails all over the floor."

"Because it's better safe than sorry."

"Hmmm. Good point."

Quentin Bertrand-Harrington was suddenly looming over them. Taj braced himself for recriminations—or worse—but instead, Quentin picked up the cake topper with his thumb and forefinger, meeting Taj's gaze. "Could we have a word?"

"Absolutely." Taj stood, but when he realized both Bernhard and Carolee were continuing to harangue Kiran, he reached out and drew the other man to his side. "With us both."

"Not so fast," Bernhard growled. "What about Annemiek's cake?

"Oh, don't worry about that," Del said, tucking their arm in Annemiek's. "I've got another one."

Chapter Twelve

At some invisible signal from Del, a trim, dark-haired man in a pink and white striped apron with *Nectar & Ambrosia* emblazoned in bold black letters on its bib bustled in, directing what seemed to be a small army of similarly aproned caterers. With his glossy curls and wide, almost black eyes, he was so ethereally beautiful that Taj would have sworn he was a member of the angelic Host if his smile weren't so mischievous. Taj had yet to meet a former angel with so much as a rudimentary sense of humor.

The man—his name tag read *Gary*—directed his catering platoon with ruthless efficiency, half of them cleaning up the mess on the floor while the other half ferried in cake tiers.

Taj and Kiran didn't have a chance to see Gary assemble the cake, though, because Quentin hauled them both into his office, the cursed cake topper still held gingerly in his hand.

"If you wouldn't mind shutting the door," Quentin said through clenched teeth, "and lift that photograph off the wall?"

Kiran pushed the door closed while Taj removed the photograph—a stunning black and white closeup of a grizzly bear standing in a stream, a trout in its big paw—to reveal a wall safe. Quentin pressed his thumb to the biometric lock, and the door swung open. He chucked the cake topper inside and slammed the safe shut. There was a muffled *fizzle-pop* from inside.

"Whew." Quentin mopped his forehead with a pristine white handkerchief. "That one was nasty." He stared at Taj severely. "I dislike having curses on the premises."

Kiran raised a tentative hand as though he were in grade school. "Then there's, um, some shoes you might want to dispose of. You can't miss them. They're red. One's in the cloakroom and the other *ought* to be buried under the left-hand bay shrub on the porch, but given that the cake topper somehow escaped anyway..." He shrugged. "Maybe the shoe did too?"

Quentin blanched. "Lucifer's balls. A curse on the threshold?" He hurried to the door and pulled it open, speaking in low tones to somebody outside. When he closed the door again and turned to them, the relief was palpable on his angular face. "My husband will take care of it. Now." He stalked over to the Aeron chair behind the desk and sat, steepling his fingers as he studied them. "Suppose you explain what just happened."

Taj shared a glance with Kiran and resolutely took his hand. "Twenty years ago—"

"I'm not asking for your life history," Quentin said irritably, "only what occurred in my ballroom ten minutes ago."

"Respectfully," Kiran said, meeting Quentin's gaze squarely, "it began twenty years ago when Naberius, Taj's progenitor, tried to curse my seven-year-old sister at the instigation of her best friend's *mother*." The disgust and anger and betrayal were clear in his tone. "He failed because I overheard them and took the curse on myself."

Quentin's eyebrows shot up above his glasses. "You did? You can't have been very old."

"Ten. But old enough to make my own choices. Naberius, however, isn't granting Taj any such option, insisting that he set the curse again. Here. Today."

"Against the same target?" Quentin leaned forward. "For the same client?"

"Yes. My sister. One of the newlyweds." Kiran glanced up at Taj with a small smile. "And he's been interfering with Taj's Upper World business, preventing students from finding his dance studio, as well as threatening both Taj and me with repercussions if Taj refused." Kiran's smile grew wider, warmer. "Which he did."

"Hmmm." Quentin tapped his fingers together. "This is illegal on so many levels." Then he grinned, and Taj startled. For such a ruggedly handsome man, Quentin's expression held shades of Naberius at his most nefarious. "Leave this to me. I'm afraid nothing can be done about the original curse, as it predated the Realm Accords. But Naberius's latest antics? He'll answer for them, you may be sure." He stood up. "Please return to the celebrations. And gentlemen?" He nodded at their joined hands. "Congratulations."

Taj shared a puzzled glance with a rather pink-cheeked Kiran, then looked back at Quentin. "I'm sorry?

Quentin ushered them to the door. "I'm an incubus. You think I can't spot a perfect match when I see one? Your auras are practically humping each other."

"*Skies*," Kiran muttered. "How mortifying. Can anyone else see?"

"Not unless they're one of the 'cubi, and I'm the only representative of my species here today."

They were almost out the door when Kiran stopped. "Quentin, what about Carolee?"

His expression turned somber. "We've informed her daughter that she's indisposed. Although the supe council has limited jurisdiction over humans, we've escorted her off the premises where she'll be subject to a memory lock. She'll be unable to contact Naberius again."

Kiran frowned. "But the fuss. Carolee's accusations. Won't the other human guests... I mean, isn't the curse reveal a violation of the Secrecy Pact?"

He chuckled. "I think you'll find that none of the humans take it seriously at all." He shooed them out the door. "Our main defense will always be innate human skepticism. Their disbelief in anything unseen or uncanny. It's one of the reasons we can hide in plain sight as we do. Enjoy your day." He closed the door, leaving them standing in the lobby, staring at one another.

That's it? It's over? Taj's chest felt three times its usual size, his heart so light that if he leaped right now, he could do a triple tour en l'air. No, a *quintuple*. Dazedly, he let Kiran lead him back to the ballroom—with a detour to the cloakroom to recover his ordinary shoes—and to the head table where, indeed, the place card next to Kiran's seat read *Taj Sekani*. Annemiek beamed at them as they sat and Del nodded, a satisfied smile on their face.

The other people at the table—Sandrine on Kiran's other side, Zeke and Hamish, as well as the newlyweds— treated Taj as though he were as much an honored guest as Kiran, with no mention at all of the Great Cake Catastrophe. True, Kiran's father kept glowering at him from his spot at the far side of the ballroom, but Taj wasn't sure whether that was cake-related or because Bernhard believed he deserved to sit at the head table himself.

With Kiran's shoulder warm against his arm as brunch progressed, course by course and toast by toast, Taj could almost believe he'd intruded on somebody else's dream. *Although if I have, I don't want to wake up.*

Sandrine's laugh brought Taj out of his reverie as the servers set slices of wedding cake in front of each of them. "Honestly," she said, "my mother is the least superstitious, most practical person I know. Well, other than you, Kiran. I can't believe she'd buy into something as ludicrous as a curse. I mean, does *anybody* believe that stuff?"

Annemiek's gaze dropped to her plate. "Ludicrous," she murmured, a catch in her voice. Del kissed her temple and she glanced up, tears glistening in her eyes.

"Oh, Anni." Sandrine turned sideways in her chair to face Annemiek. "I never knew she felt that way. I'm so, so sorry." She clasped Annemiek's hand. "I'm sorry she caused a scene. I'm sorry she betrayed your trust. I'm sorry she ever imagined I wanted your career, because I didn't. Not ever."

"I know," Annemiek whispered. "I don't blame you."

"Thank goodness." Sandrine smiled wryly at her friend. "Because I got exactly the life I wanted: you as a friend, Kiran as an honorary brother, and a front-row seat to your success. What more could I ask for?"

"What more, indeed?" Taj murmured.

"And if my mother can't accept that," Sandrine said, her tone decidedly militant, "in the future, my life will *not* include *her*."

Annemiek hugged her. "But mine will always include you, Sandy. I promise."

The two women released each other with watery chuckles, and afterward, everyone at the table was silent, forks clinking on china as they finished their cake.

Then Hamish pushed his chair back. "Sorry to run, mates, but it's showtime." He planted a smacking kiss on Zeke's mouth, which caused the shy demon to blush splotchily. "Hope you're all wearing your dancing shoes because we're going to rock this place." He stood up and bounded for the stage, where the other band members were already setting up.

When Kiran shuddered next to him, Taj draped an arm over his shoulders, still astonished that he *could*. "Worrying about a certain pair of red shoes about now?"

"Yes. Ugh. I keep imagining them tapping their way into the room and glomming onto my feet."

"You don't need to worry about that. I'm sure Quentin's slung them in his safe of destruction by now."

Kiran shook his head. "I don't know *what* I was thinking. I *knew* there had to be something sketchy about them. They were so...so relentlessly *red*."

"You were thinking you wanted your sister to be happy." Annemiek and Del swept onto the dance floor then as Hunter's Moon struck up their first tune. "And she is."

"Yes, but I should have been able to manage it with less untold pastry destruction." Kiran nestled against him, his head on Taj's shoulder. "Thank you. No matter what else went on today, I don't regret what happened in the past. I don't regret the curse. I don't regret *you*."

Heat welled behind Taj's eyes that had nothing to do with his demon nature. Could he really have all this? A life in the Upper World? His studio? Forgiveness? *Kiran?* "I'm having a hard time believing," he murmured brokenly into Kiran's silky hair, "that a former minion with so much red in his ledger could be this lucky."

Kiran tilted his head to kiss Taj's throat. "Hap."

"What?"

"Hap. It means good luck. I've considered myself pretty hapless in a lot of ways, but now, I'm feeling pretty hapful."

"Hap. I like it." Taj smiled down at him. "You know what other word comes from that same root? *Happy.* I think we're both due for a little of that, don't you?"

Kiran nodded, his eyes shining. "I do." He glanced at the guests swirling around the floor with varying degrees of grace and skill. "So." He nudged Taj's foot with his own. "Now that I'm *not* wearing cursed shoes, what do you say? May I have this dance?"

"No more nerves?"

He shook his head. "Not when I'm in your arms." He grinned. "I have it on the best authority—yours—that when you lead, you can make anyone look good. Want to prove it?"

Taj stood, drawing Kiran to his feet. "I'd like nothing more. Come along, my dear." He gave Kiran a kiss, slow and sweet, flavored with champagne and chocolate. "Let's show them what we've got."

a message from

♥ lj

Dear Reader,

Thank you so much for reading *Cursed is the Worst*. I'm so happy you've taken this journey with me! I'd be immensely grateful if you'd take a moment to leave a review at the retailer and any other site you use for reviews. Believe me, reviews make an *enormous* difference to the health and well-being of books (and not incidentally, to their associated authors!).

This novella is part of my larger Mythmatched paranormal rom-com story universe, which now comprises more than twenty stories, beginning with *Cutie and the Beast*, where a cursed fae warrior turned psychologist clashes with his determined temporary office manager. As you might expect, hi-jinks ensue! (And BTW, if you want to know where that fabulous backup cake came from, you can find out all about it in *At Odds with the Gods*, a Mythmatched/Purgatory Playhouse crossover story.)

If you're in the mood for contemporary rom-com instead, you might like *Camera Shy*, a boss/employee, fake-engagement, right-in-front-of-your-nose romantic comedy featuring a former child model-turned-PA who is *so done* with cameras, a cocky LGBTQ activist/talk show host who *does not* lose, more scarves than midwinter in Boston, and banter. So. Much. Banter.

Pop on over to my website, https://ejrussell.com, for all the deets on my books—my paranormal rom-coms and mysteries, my contemporary romances, and my one lone historical. If you're an audio fan, you can find the audio scoop there too. *Camera Shy*, for instance, is narrated by the wonderful Greg Boudreaux, and *Cutie and the Beast* by the fabulous Joel Leslie. (The QR code below will get you there with your smartphone camera or other code reader.)

Would you like exclusive content and ARC giveaways, not to mention gratuitous dance videos? Then I'd love for you to join me in E.J. Russell's Reality Optional, my Facebook fan group (https://facebook.com/groups/reality.optional). My newsletter is the place to get the latest dish on new releases, sales, and more. I promise I only send one out when I've got...well...news. You can subscribe here: https://ejrussell.com/newsletter.

All my best,
—E

Also by

ej

Paranormal Romance
Mythmatched Universe
Fae Out of Water Trilogy
Cutie and the Beast
The Druid Next Door
Bad Boy's Bard

Supernatural Selection Trilogy
Single White Incubus
Vampire With Benefits
Demon on the Down-Low

Other Mythmatched Romances
Howling on Hold
Possession in Session
Witch Under Wraps
Cursed is the Worst
The Skinny on Djinni
Assassin by Accident (part of Carnival of Mysteries)

Quest Investigations Mysteries
Five Dead Herrings
The Hound of the Burgervilles
The Lady Under the Lake
Death on Denial

At Odds with the Gods (A Mythmatched/Purgatory Playhouse crossover)

Mythmatchedlets (Mythmatched companion stories, free to newsletter subscribers in ebook form, collected in one paperback volume: *Second First Date, Rusty's Really Bad Day, First Flight, Getting the Band Together, Purgatory Postscript, A Very Quest Solstice*)

Magic Emporium Series (shared world)
Purgatory Playhouse

Enchanted Occasions Series
Best Beast
Nudging Fate
Devouring Flame

Ghost Townies Series
Ghostridden

Legend Tripping Series
Stumptown Spirits
Wolf's Clothing

Art Medium Series
The Artist's Touch
Tested in Fire
Art Medium: The Complete Collection (omnibus edition)

Royal Powers Series (shared world)
Duking It Out

Duke the Hall
King's Ex

Science Fiction
Sun, Moon, and Stars Series
Partnership
Principles

Interdimensional Time Bureau
Monster Till Midnight

Historical Romance
Silent Sin

Contemporary Romance
Camera Shy
Summer Kitchen
The Thomas Flair
Mystic Man
For a Good Time, Call… (A Bluewater Bay novel, with
Anne Tenino)

Christmas Kisses (holiday shorts)
The Probability of Mistletoe
An Everyday Hero
A Swants Soiree

Geeklandia Series
The Boyfriend Algorithm (M/F)
Clickbait

Writing as Nelle Heran

(traditional cozy mystery)

Crafty Sleuth Series (with C.K. Eastland)
Die Cut
Mixed Media
Found Objects (*coming soon*)

About the
Author

E.J. Russell (she/her), author of the award-winning Mythmatched paranormal romance series, writes LGBTQ+ romance and mystery in a rainbow of flavors. Count on high snark, low angst, and happy endings.

Reality? Eh, not so much.

She's married to Curmudgeonly Husband, a man who cares even less about sports than she does. Luckily, C.H. also loves to cook, or all three of their children (Lovely Daughter and Darling Sons A and B) would have survived on nothing but Cheerios, beef jerky, and Satsuma mandarins (the extent of E.J.'s culinary skill set).

E.J. also writes traditional cozy mystery as Nelle Heran. She lives in rural Oregon, enjoys visits from her wonderful adult children, and indulges in good books, red wine, and the occasional hyperbole.

News & Social Media:
Website: https://ejrussell.com
Newsletter: https://ejrussell.com/newsletter